NO OCEAN WIDE ENOUGH

A BEAUTIFUL, GRIPPING, AND UNFORGETTABLE WORLD WAR II NOVEL

LIVING HISTORY

FREE BONUS:
EBOOK BUNDLE

Greetings!

First of all, thank you for reading our books. As fellow passionate readers of History and Mythology, we aim to create the very best books for our readers.

Now, we invite you to join our VIP list. As a welcome gift, we offer the History & Mythology Ebook Bundle below for free. Plus you can be the first to receive new books and exclusives! <u>Remember it's 100% free to join.</u>

Simply scan the QR code to join.

NO OCEAN WIDE ENOUGH

Chapter One

Eddie
June 2, 1944

"—eh, Eddie?"

The jaunty wail of a saxophone and the soft, slow beat of a radio tune melt away as my dream evaporates. The hazy image of a smoke-filled club back in New York City morphs into the dull roar of the ocean. My eyes remain closed as I slowly regain my bearings. Instead of the wooden floor of the nightclub, I'm squeezed between Johnny and Lawrie in the long line of boys seated around the mess hall, now turned into temporary quarters.

Ah yes, I sigh. *Right. We're trapped in a rusty*

bucket making our way down to some beach in France. Unlike other, luckier companies, ours had to move its initial spot on deck to the mess hall.

With the bad weather, I wasn't complaining. *It could be better*, I remind myself, *but it could be worse.*

Another sharp shove against my shoulder draws my gaze over to the right. Johnny is in the middle of an animated discussion with some of the other boys.

"No shut-eye for you," Lawrie says, lighting another smoke and offering his lighter wordlessly.

Within a minute, I'm leaning back with a contented sigh, exhaling a cloud of smoke. Whatever nerves I might have had seemed to be calming down.

"I was dreaming of New York," I admit quietly. "Or maybe it was a nightclub in Paris...

Something like that."

"Hm," Lawrie grunts, "I don't imagine the Frenchies are kicking it up in a club these days."

"No. I know." I wince, imagining that one club in Paris now buried under a pile of rubble. "Probably end up a pile of rubble now between us and the Jerries."

"If we don't get there, the Russkies will," Lawrie says, shaking his head.

Lawrence Johnson, better known to most as Lawrie, is a solid, broad-shouldered man. Quiet and saturnine, Lawrie rarely talks, but in these moments, I have to admit that his presence is reassuring. Running his hands through his dark hair, Lawrie shakes his head and casts a glance beyond me. Johnny Garland, leaning back and laughing, slaps down his hand of cards, causing the other card players to groan. Mattie O'Keefe cusses up a blue storm, much to the hilarity of Vinny Smith, who throws his own hand down with a short chuckle.

"Come on, Eddie! You oughta jump in here and help a man out," Vinny begs, catching sight of my amused look.

"Eddie is a cautious man," Johnny chuckles. "I'd think twice before taking on Ed. You two wanna go?"

"Spending what might be the last few days of my life losing at cards?" Lawrie shakes his head. "No thank you."

"Good God, Lawrie." Mattie rolls his eyes.

"There's the Lawrie we know," Johnny says with a laugh.

His laughter, drowned out by a sudden burst of wind and waves, cuts off as our gazes drift to the small porthole above my head. The gray light pouring in darkens as the boat founders and the port side submerges beneath what must have been a great wave. For a moment, the floor slants. Lawrie shoots Mattie a look. It reminds me of the look my mother would give me back when I'd come home with torn pants after roughhousing on the street.

Mother. Drew. Callie. The thought of my family brings up old memories... and more recent ones. I can't help but wonder what they are doing now. The day I was drafted, Drew had fallen silent—knowing that it would have been him if I hadn't been chosen. Only one of us was allowed to remain. Mother had lost Father in the first war already, so it only made sense that Drew, now married and a father of two young children, would stay home.

It had been an easy choice for me. Still, Mother had cried, and Callie, ever practical, had announced her intentions to volunteer even more of her spare time to the war effort. I tried to reassure them. After all, this was my choice. I had my reasons. Now, like Lawrie, I found myself caught up in a storm I can barely comprehend.

"Someone has to say it," Lawrie says, drawing on

his cigarette and exhaling a long stream of smoke. "Anyone wants to bet that we'll all be back here playing cards in a week's time?"

"I can only hope so," Mattie replies, picking up the cards Johnny deals out. "You were saying that we're probably not headed for Calais, Eddie? Wasn't that your prediction?"

"I hold to it," I maintain stoutly.

"Denny told me that the bearings are definitely not for Calais," Lawrie interjects.

"Denny?" asks Vinny.

Elvin—better known as Vinny—is the youngest in our group. Barely out of school and still wet behind the years in more ways than one, Vinny has often boasted about his repeated failed attempts to join up before he turned eighteen. He signed on as soon as he reached his majority a month ago and recently arrived in Belfast. Wide-eyed and ready for anything, Vinny is always pestering us with questions. Lawrie and

I, who feel like old men next to Vinny, step in to help the kid more often than not.

"Radio operator," Lawrie explains.

"They'd know, I suppose," Johnny agrees.

"Normandy or the Cotentin Peninsula," I reiterate. "Just a hunch though."

"Con-ten-teen," Vinny repeats after me, attempting and failing to achieve the proper accent.

"Co-tawn-tan," I correct him with a smile. "The 'n' is—"

"Oh god, Eddie," Mattie says and rolls his eyes. "Are we to get a French lesson now?"

"Better now than the last minute before we hit Paris," Johnny points out.

"Paris?" asked Vinny.

"Where Johnny thinks the real ladies are," Lawrie explains, giving Johnny an indulgent look.

Since we left America, Johnny had been spinning yarns about the ladies on the Continent, and the Irish lookers had certainly lived up to some of his tales. Johnny, the tallest, blondest, and most blue-eyed man in the company, had caught a lot of eyes back in Ireland. No doubt he'd left behind a fair few broken hearts. When Vinny joined up, he'd been impressed by Johnny's gaggle of girls, much to the amusement of Lawrie and me.

"Already forgotten the poor Irish girls?" Mattie asks.

"I can remember them all." Johnny crooks a smile in my direction. "But I fancy that Eddie will do really well. With all that French under his belt. And he's visited Paris before."

"Before the war?" asks Vinny.

"Yes," I reply. "Fresh out of college, I thought a trip to Paris would be a fair treat after my studies. Back then, I was on a straight track to translation work with a publishing house... or the government. But the war changed a lot of that. Now here we are."

"Here we are," Lawrie echoes softly, his words barely audible beneath another crash of waves. "Headed to God knows where."

"Normandy," I correct him.

"How many Jerries do you think are waiting?" Mattie wonders aloud.

"Too many," Lawrie predicts pessimistically.

Glancing over at the grave look that flits across Vinny's face, I fancy that the storm and the past two nights spent on a ship in such close quarters might be weighing on him. Back home, the idea of fighting for God and country, toting a gun, sweeping a lady off her feet, returning home decorated—all of that might have felt like the perfect adventure to a young man. Reality is something else altogether.

"When you get back home, what do you plan to do?" I ask everyone, hoping to steer the conversation away from what faces us ahead.

At my question, the group falls silent. Beyond, other huddled groups of men continue talking and quietly joking. Vinny stares down at the hand of cards dealt to him and shuffles thoughtfully. Mattie glares at Johnny and throws his hand down with another curse. Lawrie stubs out his smoke and exhales deeply.

"Sleep," Lawrie finally answers.

"I've got a family farm that'll need a hand, I reckon," Mattie sighs. "Not the most exciting, but after the war, it might be what I need."

"My mum wanted me to go into a factory," Vinny says. "Car manufacturing is what I was hoping for, or working with cars, as a mechanic."

"Not a bad idea." Johnny shrugs. "I was in an advertising company, writing copy for newspapers and advertisements. Hopefully, the old place will still be going when I get back. How about you, Eddie?"

"Get back to what I was planning," I reply. "I was contracted to a publishing house, but I could go into teaching, although I was hoping to find a government job somewhere. Find the right girl for me, settle down... white picket fence and all that."

"Perhaps you'll find someone in Paris," Vinny suggests, glancing at Johnny in a vain attempt to keep casual about his hand.

Johnny knows Vinny's tells and folds, much to the younger man's disappointment. The win is small, but Vinny still shows off his straight flush. Johnny claps Vinny on the back.

At the thought of Paris, I lean back. Some of the men are bedding down for a short sleep. Between the wind and the waves, I can barely hear the other men's chatter. Vinny shuffles and deals out the cards again. Lawrie settles in beside me and hums to himself, no doubt in an effort to calm his nerves. I close my eyes and think about my dreams.

Sure, fighting the Jerries is important. After the invasion of France four years ago, many of us knew that the Nazis were going to pose a real threat to the world. Then Pearl Harbor was bombed. That day, I knew that President Roosevelt would be calling on us to do our duty, not just as Americans but as citizens of the free world. This war would determine the future of the entire globe. That much had been clear to me.

But there were other reasons, other memories. Images of Paris, of the Eiffel Tower towering overhead, and of the call of a bright voice drawing my gaze away. It had been a gloomy day, roaming the Jardin de la Tour Eiffel alone, but then Amélie arrived. That had brightened up my entire day. Memories of those moments remain with me even now—the lilt of her laughter, her effusive gestures, the press of her hand in the crook of my elbow as I escorted her about the gardens. After almost five years of separation, the promises we made to each other remain. I need to find Amélie. First, I just have to survive one of the most significant battles we have yet to face, the one they are calling D-Day.

Chapter Two

Amélie
June 2, 1944

For the fifth time, I peek out of our kitchen window, drawing the thin blue cotton curtain back just a little. Gazing up at the treeline, I watch the clouds scud past. The trees on the edge of the yard toss their branches uneasily. It has been raining steadily for the past few days, but a break in the weather has raised my hopes. With everything that has been happening lately, hope feels like a rare treasure.

"The rain will be back, Amélie. Before the night falls, it'll be coming down again as thick as ever." My mother's voice breaks into my thoughts, and I draw back from the window, letting the curtain fall back.

Stifling a sigh, I turn away and move over to the ancient stove, where I fuss over the kettle slowly warming up over the open fire I built beneath. A few years ago, we had gas, but the war effort has long since deprived us of what we had once considered essential.

All that has changed, I muse. *Now we know what we can live without... If you can call this living.*

The water starts to bubble cheerfully. I lift the kettle and carefully fill my mother's best ceramic teapot, the one with the blue-and-white glazed painting. Imported from Belgium by my grandmother half a century ago, my mother always says. It is one of the few things left to my parents. I pull out four plain teacups while I allow the tea to steep on the kitchen table. I am able to add a few dollops of milk to the red tea, but our sugar has long since run out. Setting out a couple of dry biscuits, I make up a tray for my mother and father. It's not much, but it might provide a little bit of cheer on this gloomy afternoon.

At the sound of a soft rap on the kitchen's back door, I glance over at my mother, wipe my hands on the apron tied about my waist, and peek out the kitchen window again. It's Dottie, right on schedule. With a sigh of relief, I make my way over to the door and let my bosom friend in.

"Come in, come in," I say warmly, tension easing out of my shoulders. "I was rather worried."

"I know," Dorothée groans with a put-upon sigh. "I came as soon as I could. I'd have been here earlier, but the Nazi-loving pig caught me on our front walk and of course had to brag about his recent assignment for the Commander."

"Albert Moulin, ever the bully," Mama says severely. She rises to her feet and takes the tray I have finished preparing. "I remember that boy when he was only knee-high. Vicious and cruel... and had a bad habit of kicking people in the shins. I suppose some people never change. Well, I'll leave you two girls to it. I'm sure your papa is wondering where his tea is."

With that, Mama makes her way out of the kitchen. Once she has left with the biscuits and tea, I pour a cup for Dottie and sit down opposite her, cupping my own steaming brew. I give Dottie a once-over. Despite her plain brown skirt, sensible white blouse, and threadbare button-up jacket, the twinkle in Dottie's eye and her healthy complexion would be sure to draw any man's eye for miles around, including Albert. There aren't that many young women like ourselves in the countryside at any rate, which no doubt makes things worse.

Still, Dottie chooses to fight back. She is still the same courageous girl I had known as a childhood friend. Despite the long passage of years that separated us before the war, after I returned home we soon discovered that we shared similar beliefs about the war and the German occupation. As 'dissidents,' 'traitors,' and other supposed 'undesirables' disappeared, we had both begun to fear for the future of our country. Would we one day disappear as well? Still, despite our feelings, we barely understood the part we could play. Thankfully, Dottie's brother introduced us to his friend Louis and since then, the two of us have found ways to help the Resistance effort. It is a dangerous road to walk, but I would choose no other.

"I encouraged him, of course," Dottie assures me. "Albert spilled everything, so eager was he to impress. Honestly, it is rather pathetic... but at least we have a better idea about the situation. You will pass on the news to Louis?"

"What news do you have?" I ask, lowering my voice to a whisper, my gaze instantly flitting to the window as though expecting Albert or one of the Nazi officers on patrol to suddenly appear. "Is there any explanation about the patrols up in Caen?"

"Not just Caen, unfortunately. There is a

movement about Calais," Dottie whispers. "And it looks as though it will remain so for some time. Even the nearby fishing villages along the coast have come under heavy surveillance. The pig Führer is worried."

"Our worst nightmare has come true, then," I mutter. "There is no chance for us to take Rachel and her son to England through the north."

"No," Dottie replies, her pale blue eyes now shadowed with worry. "Even worse, we can expect more patrols and battalions coming through Caen. You remember old Father Paul...?"

"Father Paul?" I say, squinting in thought.

It has been a good year since I've been able to attend Mass.

"Well, he's the last priest remaining at Saint-Étienne-le-Vieux," Dottie reminds me. "One of the last few in this region."

"Ah! Yes!" I smile at a distant memory of a

biking trip Dottie and I had made to Caen at the start of the war. "Before our bicycles were commandeered, yes. We went shopping, picked up those documents for Louis... and we went to Mass at the cathedral. Such a lovely time."

"Now the church lies empty, but Father Paul refuses to leave. He told my contact that Caen is shuttered and Allied planes have been flying over the region sporadically. The panzer divisions have been mobilized, but Albert told me that the worst of it will be to the north."

"Did he say why?" I ask.

"He said..." Dottie leans forward, gripping her teacup. "He said that the Führer believes the British and their allies will strike against Calais. The Allies have been running bombing raids over Calais lately."

"Calais..." I echo softly as the image of the coastal city rises in my mind.

A long time ago, when life was easier and our

days beneath the sun had been more filled with joy, my mother and father had taken me to Calais for a short trip. The ocean was not much different from what I had seen on the Cotentin Peninsula's beaches, but the number of attractions a young person could enjoy had been diverse. It had been a time of exploration and constant enjoyment. Those days have long since faded into the past.

Newer, fonder memories of my adventures in Paris still haunt me, however. The adventure of starting school in the big city had felt like a dream come true. But the opportunity to study fashion had battled with the distractions of Paris—the lure of dance halls, night cafes, and tea socials. I don't have the time anymore to daydream about those moments spent by the Seine with my school friends... with Eddie. It is better to focus on the here and now, on the challenges of life in a country wracked by war.

Do I regret my choices? No, I decide. *I would choose no other, but Rachel and her son never chose this. Their lives are threatened by the simple fact that they were born Jewish. After everything they've been through, is there nothing we can do to help them escape to safety and freedom?*

"With Calais under heavy occupation, another path will need to be found," I finally say. "I wonder what Louis will think. Sometimes I fancy he has contact with the British. Perhaps he'd know the truth... but either way, Rachel and her son will not be able to travel north."

"They will not be able to travel anywhere," Dottie says, "and certainly not together. They will have to be separated. I saw another patrol on my walk over to your house. And Caen's streets are filled with German soldiers."

"We can send the boy to a farm and hide him amongst a large family. His papers could suggest that he is a cousin... " I muse slowly. "As for Rachel, she could continue living in the shed for a short time, but perhaps we could find another passage further south, along the coast."

"There are divisions moving along the beaches of Normandy, are there not?" asked Dottie.

"Last I heard, there is a handful," I admit. "Louis will have a better idea, though. If Normandy is closed off—"

I come to an abrupt halt as I hear a distant whine and then its accompanying rumbles. Our eyes move to the kitchen windows. With the sun setting, any ray of light will become a target. Quickly, the two of us go through the familiar ritual of blacking out the windows, drawing the shutters, and pulling thick curtains closed. We return to the kitchen with a sigh, but Dottie remains standing this time. Instead, she makes her way over to the back door and peers out.

The trees are now swaying under a heavier wind and large droplets fall as the storm from the coast moves inland. Overhead, the clouds move swiftly, and in between the cloud cover I fancy I catch sight of a formation of planes as it dips down and races to the west. I fold my arms defensively and shiver a little under the shawl I pull closer around my shoulders.

"The storm is moving," Dottie notes, looking up at the sky, with its thick purple-gray clouds hiding the setting sun. Her face wrinkles with a frown. "I'm going back."

"Not just the storm," I reply wryly. "If it isn't the rain, it's the bombs dropping on our heads. We'll be sleeping in our cellar tonight."

"Yes. Be safe, Amélie." Dottie draws on her coat, her fingers flying over the buttons. She turns to give me a long look. Neither of us wants to make the goodbye more than it is, but certainly, an ill-timed bomb could end anyone tonight.

"You too, Dottie," I say softly, giving her a quick hug.

"Tomorrow, you will see Louis?"

"Yes," I nod, refusing to dwell on the uncertainty we face. "Tomorrow. I will pass on the news about the coast and Calais. As well as Albert's ramblings. I'm certain we will find a way for Rachel and little Joseph."

"Let's hope so," Dottie replies.

With that, she slips out into the falling night. I close the door and snuff all but one of the candles. In the dim silence, I quickly wash up the dishes before rejoining my parents in the cellar below.

Chapter Three

Eddie
June 6, 1944

At some point, we must have arrived at our destination despite the weather. The ship gunnery begins to pound the beach with regularity, and overhead I can hear the whine of distant airplanes. It's not just fighter pilots but also the larger ones carrying men trained in parachuting, I can hear Lawrie tell Vinny. Our boys will hopefully drop inland safely and skirmish in the countryside, disrupting communication between the enemy battalions.

I squint down at my wristwatch, which is an exercise in futility thanks to the morning darkness. Half of the mess hall has been cleared.

Mattie and Johnny have rejoined their companies, leaving Lawrie, Vinny, and I with the rest of ours. The party is over, and the real work has begun. It reminds me of the moment when I waved farewell to a handful of other servicemen I met in Belfast. The group had parted ways vowing to meet again one day—a kind of cheerful bravado in the face of what we were heading into.

The specifics of the battle haven't been shared with us, of course. Lawrie and I both think Churchill and Eisenhower are hoping to give Hitler a shock. I look over at Vinny, who tries to say something. But between the regular boom of the guns, the waves pounding against the ship, and the patter of rain, I can barely hear anything else. Judging by the jostling and heaving of the ship, the storm has not passed, but the call for formation is going out regardless.

Vinny nudges me and points wordlessly at the line of men forming in front of the doors. Since I had double-checked my kit the night before, preparations are swift. Glancing over, I can see Lawrie already lounging in line, working through a smoke. He catches my eye and jerks his head. As I make my way over to his side, I glance out one of the portholes and note the vague lightening of the sky.

"Our time's up," Lawrie raises his voice a little so as to be heard. He offers me half his smoke. "They had some trouble with getting our landing craft ready, but it's ready now, I think."

"The rest?" I ask.

"Gone," Lawrie replies.

"Any word?" I raise an eyebrow.

"You mean, any wounded return?" Lawrie shakes his head. "None that I've seen. What I do know is that you win the bet. Not that there really was one."

"The beach in Normandy," I sigh. "A long, flat stretch of ground sloping up, and Jerries sitting back taking potshots at the boys coming in."

"You forgot the part about the mines as well," Lawrie adds.

A high-pitched whistle sounds and the line slowly begins to move down the hall to the gangway and then up and out. After fifteen minutes of shuffling, I finally reach the deck. Everyone and their aunt is packed together and looking up at Colonel Jim, who's looking through binoculars to the north. I follow his gaze beyond the port side of our ship and can't help but notice another ship flying our colors. It, too, is lined with two or three landing craft—now jam-packed with men.

"Second wave, I think." Lawrie's drawl catches my attention. "We're going to be the third wave, I guess. Dunno whether that's gonna be a good or bad thing."

"If the Jerries have run out of ammo... Good?" I suggest.

"We'll find out soon enough." Lawrie turns to squint over the rough waves toward the coast.

A short speech begins. We are briefed about what we face, our objective, and what role our win will have in the war. This is D-Day, the day the Americans, British, and Canadians will gain a foothold on the western coast of Europe. Once our place is secured, we will be able to make a road to Berlin and take on Hitler himself.

"Many of you boys, maybe even half of you, won't be making it home tonight," our briefer tells us.

Hearing it spoken so bluntly gives most of us pause. Now that the explosions burst unmuffled, now that the sight of smoke and wire-festooned beaches lies before our eyes, the words hit particularly hard. Even the younger men, many of them not yet having reached their twentieth year, look a little apprehensive as we finally make our way down the nets into the open landing craft.

I find a seat toward the back, where I can peer over the edge out towards the smoky line of the beach. Then the engines start to rev up, and we chug toward the beach now designated 'Omaha.' I suppress a shudder as I think about the hellscape that certainly lies ahead.

Line after line of planes, most of them American, drop their cargo, sending up plumes of smoke, sand, and debris in the wake of ground-shaking explosions. A wave suddenly slams against the boat and obscures my view as the small transport craft rocks dangerously from side to side. A few of the men are already getting sick and throwing up in their helmets. The rest of us look green, trying to hold back rising nausea.

Between the sounds and the tension, the journey feels like it lasts forever, but eventually we arrive. After coming to a grinding halt in the surf, we sway from the shock of the jolt and the pounding waves. We are still a good way off from the actual beach. The rest of the way, we will have to wade. Despite the fact that we are no longer in open water, the force of the waves still pummels us. The storm winds have whipped the waves up larger, and they nearly batter aside the gangplank as it falls forward and down into the water.

"Take care with the waves. Disembark off the side of the plank or directly off the boat," someone is shouting. "Head inland to the designated point."

I don't need to be told. It's clear to me that the gangplank is the least stable point of exit, and it's also enthusiastically being targeted by machine-gun fire from the coast. Following Lawrie, I manage to find a way over the side of the craft, all too aware of the bullets chipping away on either side of me. Once I hit the cold water, my body suddenly seems to wake up to a whole new level of awareness.

Whether it is the tension, the fear, the reverberations from the artillery blasts, or the knowledge we are racing into certain death, I find myself suddenly hyper-alert and awake. I move forward slowly now, shoulder to shoulder with Lawrie.

I'm drenched to the waist and my equipment is heavy with water, but I keep going. For the past six months, I had spent almost every moment of my time training for battle, and, remembering the orders and signals, my body now responds automatically. Although the weight is cumbersome, I somehow manage to make my way to shore.

Like Lawrie, I keep my head down. We grimly push past the floating corpses of servicemen and make our way to the sandy, flat shore. After all of those planes flying overhead, I had rather thought the beach would be full of craters, but I don't see massive holes or the bodies of Jerries like I expected. Most of the Jerry soldiers are hunkered down on the low hills surrounding the beach, hidden among the greenery. Our boys, coming in off the boat, are easy targets.

There's no time to talk. Lawrie and I run

forward, drop down, and then rise to run forward again as we make our way to a small pocket of sand, where we catch our breath. Whatever kind of order had existed on the boat has long since disappeared. The men make their way forward as best they can. Any memory of a target point for our offense has long since disappeared; our focus narrows to simply finding some kind of shelter against the rain of bullets that shower around us.

I assume the entire shore up to the embankment from which the Jerries are firing is littered with mines, but it's clear from the bodies of the men in the first regiments where the worst of the danger lies. Our pace picks up as we follow the lines of men, trying not to trip over the dead. Someone ahead of us falls. Lawrie and I, stooping lower, duck and shift to the left. It's Dan. Dan is a cashier from Virginia. Dead, God help him. He has fallen beside another man who has been dead for a good hour or so. Lawrie quickly makes the sign of the cross and keeps moving forward, jaw set. Others are screaming for help, but we know better than to stop and check.

Looking ahead, I notice the welcome sight of a large hole in the ground. Lawrie, as if reading my mind, stoops low and bolts toward it. Only a few feet away from the shelter, I realize that someone else has fallen and is trying to crawl further forward, clearly wounded.

Oh God, it's Vinny. Jerking on Lawrie's arm, I point wordlessly. Nodding sharply, he follows me closely. Pulling the young man up and slinging his arms around our shoulders, we drag him forward to a semi-sheltered dugout, where a group of men has found a safe place to entrench themselves. It is a sight better than the exposed portion of the beach, but at any moment a shell or mortar could land on us and kill everyone in an instant.

Men with shovels are piling more sand on the small embankment and widening it to make room for others who manage to straggle in. Looking back, I suppress the chill that rises at the sight of all the bodies, lying newly dead on the beach. A blood trail leads into the dugout from where we had dragged Vinny. There's no time to panic. Surrounded by the whine of bullets and the roar of explosions, we gently help Vinny lie down and investigate the broadening patch of blood that now soaks his entire leg.

"Medic?" I shout. "Is there a medic?"

My voice is drowned out by incoming fire, but someone must have heard because I get the discouraging response: "Another one's coming!"

"They're gone," Neil says, hunkering down beside me. "I'm the new squad captain. Tom went down... among others. If we're lucky, we'll get reinforcements and medics soon. Either way, the wounded stay and we press forward to the seawall. That will offer some protection. Maybe we can find an officer who knows what to do next."

I nod, deciding to focus on the simple tourniquet I'm now cinching around the kid's leg. Vinny, thank God, has passed out. If he's lucky, he'll remain unconscious as he bleeds out. Pressing several wads of cloth against the gaping wound on Vinny's thigh, I tie down the bandages. They are soaked in blood instantly. Lawrie drags off Vinny's pack and pushes it underneath his leg.

"I heard something about elevating helping," he explains.

"It's as much as we can do," I sigh.

Vinny's eyes drag open for a moment and, catching sight of my face, he smiles. I force a smile in return and meet his gaze with a show of encouragement.

"You keep awake, Vinny, and the doc will be here to help you out. Just gotta keep awake," I repeat. "You hear me. You've still got a few Jerries to take out."

"Roger that," Vinny chokes out. His lips are tinged red with blood.

God knows what other injuries he sustained from the bullet or shell that caught him. No doubt he's bleeding internally, but I'm not a medic. The best I can do is hope. Waiting isn't even an option. Despite having lost a third of our company, we are to press forward and make our way further in, where the earlier vanguards have found a seawall to hunker down in. Pressing an abandoned jacket beneath Vinny's head, I repeat my instructions. Vinny closes his eyes. I squeeze his shoulder in comfort and sit back on my heels, wondering how long it will take for reinforcements to arrive.

"The wounded are remaining here." Lawrie rejoins me. His mouth is a thin line of repressed emotion. "Most of them can't walk further. If a medic can be spared up ahead, they'll come back. We have to press on. Orders are orders."

"I know," I reply huskily. "Let's go then."

As I move forward with the others, I can't help but wonder whether I'll ever see Vinny again.

Chapter Four

Amélie
June 6, 1944

The early morning sky is a dull pale blue in the east, but the horizon to the west seems to glow fiery red. Overhead, planes buzz low, circling around and around. I catch a glimpse of two planes flying toward each other amid flashes of light. A dogfight. For a moment, I pause and watch with bated breath as the German plane begins to smoke and spirals downward. The other plane, no doubt recognizing the inevitable death of its enemy, speeds northward.

Returning to our back door, I stop to listen, straining to hear any sound—a distant explosion, the sound of gunfire, or the shouts of soldiers. There's nothing... yet. I quickly finish up a small breakfast of an egg, a piece of toast, and two cups of tea. Mama and Papa, emerging from the cellar, assure me that they can handle breakfast on their own.

After all these years, the two remain stubbornly independent. Back before the Great War, Papa had worked with the police force in Caen but then retired to manage the family farm when his older brother passed on. Since then, my parents have enjoyed the relative quiet of the French countryside. That all changed when the Germans came. The Krauts, my father often calls them. As a retired police officer, he was contacted by the Germans when they arrived. Since then, Papa has been forced to resume some of his previous duties. Some nights, he comes home looking grimmer—and drunk— than usual.

"I could have sworn I heard the planes all night," Papa grunts. "Something is afoot. I can feel it in my bones."

"Certainly, there have been more soldiers about," Mama says. She glances over at me with mild curiosity, patting her white hair back into a loose bun. "Did Dottie have any news, Amélie?"

"Some," I reply cautiously, wondering how much to tell them. "Albert told her that the Germans are massing to the north in preparation for an invasion. It should be any day now."

"Calais? Or north of it," Papa says. "If the Krauts think it is Calais, I hope to God the Allies think twice before striking."

"Would any coastline in France be safe?" Mama wonders.

"I think not," I reply. "But I think we will need to be careful regardless. Perhaps it would be better to move further into the countryside. We could go visit Pierre—"

"No, no," Papa shakes his head. "I am not moving for the Krauts or anyone else for that matter."

"We are quite decided on it," Mama said. "Besides, Antoine and Bea told us we could use their shelter should the bombs get much worse."

"Just be careful." I force a smile.

Leaning in to give my parents a peck on the cheek and quick hugs, I keep my voice light.

"I will be out for the day," I tell them, pulling on a shawl and hat. "Dottie and I have a small visit to make. A picnic perhaps."

"If anyone is to be careful, it is you," my mother replies. "Going out and about when bombs are dropping and soldiers are patrolling!"

The image of the faint red sky to the west sends a shiver down my spine, but I keep my face neutral as I listen to my parents' gentle scolding. Repeating promises to return home for dinner, I slip out and make my way down the road to Dottie's family cottage. My gaze fixes on the tree line and the pink, smoky hue of the brightening sky beyond. That way, I know, lies Normandy. Has something happened on the beaches?

A few days ago, I met with Louis and told him the news Dottie had passed on to me. His response had been quiet, as though he knew something. If he was aware of any plans, the tight-lipped Resistance fighter didn't tell me. I knew better than to press the subject. After all, the less I know, the less of a liability I am. I listened instead to his plans for Rachel and Joseph Friedmann and agreed to meet again in a few days. Dottie and I are to escort Joseph to his new family while Rachel travels further south to a small fishing village below the Peninsula. That is the plan. How well it will go is anyone's guess.

Knocking on Dottie's front door, I am ushered into the front room where Dottie, her sister Janine, and her sister's husband Rémy sit. The two don't pry about our trip to the back fields, but Rémy is eager to talk about the red sky he had seen early in the morning when he'd gone out to milk the few cows they had left. The increase in planes sweeping across the countryside, the bombing, and the sight of German patrols actively increasing on the road to Caen had everyone speculating.

"We are thinking of going further in," Rémy says, glancing at the windows again apprehensively. "Perhaps Paris... or Le Mans."

"Is there any way to escape the fighting, though?" I wonder. "Perhaps if we manage to get through the worst of it, we might be freed by the Allies."

"If they are coming from Calais as Albert said, it will be some time," Janine sighs.

"Not that Albert's prediction is correct," Dottie points out. "He only knows what the Germans know, nothing more. If the red sky is any indication, my guess is that they are attempting to take Normandy. Caen should be freed soon after."

"Either way, we shall have to be careful," Janine says. "There are the bombs to worry about, the safety of our shelter… and the question of food stores."

"As long as we work together, I am certain we can find a way to survive," I reply. "We will do our best to make sure that as many people as possible come out the other side, right, Dottie?"

"Even if we end up only helping our neighbors," Dottie says grimly, "I will consider my duty done."

"You'd best get going, then," Rémy says. "Time is not on our side."

With that, Dottie finishes packing up our picnic basket, and we are off. The yard, once a well-tended garden, has long since gone wild and degenerated into an unkempt thicket of flowers, grass, and dirt. Below, Rémy has built an underground shelter, hoping to protect his family against the worst of the bombs. The ramp pointed away from the house, leads toward the narrow footpath running behind the row of houses.

Pulling my shawl more tightly around my shoulders, I follow Dottie along the line of trees. Around us, the farmland is divided into square fields, lined with hedges, ditches, and roads as well as trees. Anyone could get lost if they were not familiar with the area, but Dottie and I know all of the secret paths and hidden nooks in the fields. Eventually, we reach the small toolshed where Rachel and her son have been hiding for the past two weeks.

Drawing close, we see Louis smoking a pipe by the thick stand of trees near the shed. Beside him, a small battered truck filled with farming supplies and cargo stands at the ready. I recognize Henri, another Resistance member, at the wheel. Behind him, a woman sits by Rachel. Glancing over at us, Louis gives us a small nod. The man's hardened, craggy features lighten only a little at the sight of our approach. To any passersby, we might look like two frivolous ladies stopping to ask some farmers about the weather. That is what I hope, at any rate.

"The skies were red in the west this morning," I tell him.

"I heard," Louis says as he exhales a stream of smoke and glares up at the sky. "But we can't wait. Not with the patrols increasing. The other day..." He shakes his head. "They are looking through toolsheds now. And not just for Jews, mind you. Anything metal that can be melted for bullets. Or runaways, perhaps. Deserters. There are those as well."

The truck's engine turns over once or twice. In the distance, the whine of a plane overhead and a distant blast raises the hair on my arms. Dottie also looks unsettled.

"Is he ready?" Dottie asks, no doubt feeling the same sense of urgency that washes over me.

"He is." Louis knocks out his pipe and disappears into the tool shed.

After a few seconds, he re-emerges with a young boy in tow. Joseph Friedmann, eight years old, looks frightened and teary-eyed. He has no doubt just said goodbye to his mother. At the sight of the car, his dark eyes widen, but his lips press closed. My hand reaches around his thin trembling shoulders in silent comfort. I wish I could promise him the world, that his mother would be safe, that they would meet again, but nothing can take away his grief.

"We'd best get going," Dottie finally says in a hushed voice. "The side path should take us there."

"Let's go, Joseph." I squeeze his shoulders gently and take the pack Louis offers me.

"His papers are in the front pocket," Louis says.

"Right." I nod.

With that, the three of us cross the road, squeeze through an invisible cutting in the hedge, and then cut across the fields, keeping out of sight of the main road. The truck is now a dot on the horizon, but it is joined by another blur. I freeze as the truck comes to a stop.

"What is it?" Dottie asks, voice falling to a whisper.

"A patrol," I reply. "It should miss us. And I'm certain the papers will pass muster."

Peeking back over the edge, I notice that Louis has already gotten on his weather-beaten bicycle. He usually turns in the opposite direction, toward Paris, but this time he seems to be waiting, gazes fixed on the road. A gust of wind carries the distant sound of shouting. A door slams. A gun fires. More shouting, and then two more gunshots. Silence falls.

At the shots, I duck almost automatically and then press the hedge leaves aside to see how Louis will respond. The man's gaze fixes on my own only briefly, his dark eyes filled with sadness and anguish, but there is no time to talk. Casually, he turns and makes his way down the east road. Dropping down, I draw Joseph close and gaze over the young boy's head at Dottie, fighting my rising panic. Had the three of them just been killed? What happened? Would Louis be safe? How are we to get to Joseph's next stop with suspicious Germans patrolling everywhere? Suddenly, our return home felt more uncertain than ever.

Chapter Five

Eddie
June 6, 1944

After eight hours of crawling, bending, and dodging enemy fire about the edges of the beach, I am shaking with exhaustion and pent-up tension. The seawall initially offers a reprieve, but as the hours tick by, it becomes increasingly clear that we cannot stay hidden behind the wall forever. Looking down the stretch of beach that we have managed to cross, I'm mesmerized by the sight of all the bodies. The ones rolling in the surf, the ones who have fallen on the sand... and the wounded who still cry out for help.

It makes me wonder about the sandy crater

where we left Vinny and the others. Have they survived? God only knows. Still, there is no way we can go back. There is only one way—forward. Turning around, I carefully look to my right at the distant edge of the embankments overhead. The Jerries are sitting nice and comfy in their bunkers, shooting from their pillboxes, while our boys, damp and scared and miserable, wondering how we are ever going to get up there.

Next to me, Lawrie pulls out his lighter and a cigarette. His hands shake a little, but he finally manages to light it. After the first inhale, he slouches down and focuses his gaze grimly out at the Atlantic. No doubt he feels just about as unsteady and worn as I do, but the chance for rest seems to have settled him. Wordlessly, he holds out half of his smoke, and I take it with a nod of thanks. If the explosions, the pounding surf, and the rattle of bullets weren't so loud, I might have thought this was just another one of our quiet times spent together. After the first inhale, I feel a little better. That's not saying much, but it's better than nothing. I have much to be thankful for. I could be Vinny. I could be our sergeant, lying dead somewhere in the surf. I could be that incoming transport craft, already smoking and battered by incoming fire.

I glance over at the rest of the men, who sit with their backs against the seawall. Neil is moving further down the wall, no doubt looking for alternative routes toward the cliff. The rest of us wait uneasily. Now that we've arrived, I can't help but wonder: *Is this it?* When we were told to join the vanguard, I thought there would be more. There is barely anyone left.

Perhaps, like us, there are other pockets of men, hiding in craters or dugouts in the sand. Perhaps a few have made it past the seawall to the bottom of the cliff. *But even if we get there, even if we join up... What are we going to do?* I wonder. *Without any real leadership, with no armor or tanks or proper guns, it feels like we're just waiting to die.* Pinned down as we are, our movement is limited. Bullets chip endlessly against the edges of the seawall. One of the boys, raising his head to look beyond, falls back dead in an instant. No one tries to look across the wall after that.

Further down the seawall, I can hear someone shouting faintly. Has someone been wounded? Did more reinforcements arrive? Someone else, closer to us, starts shouting as well. It's hard to parse the exact words, but the tone is definitely one of excitement. Lawrie and I glance at each other in confusion.

"It's Cota!" the man on Lawrie's right yells to us.

"Cota arrived?" someone further down from us yells back for confirmation.

"The Major General has arrived!" the man repeats.

"It's our chance, boys!" someone else cheers.

My heart leaps a little at the news. If Major General Cota has truly arrived, then perhaps we have a fighting chance. A few minutes later, a soldier approaches us. Judging by the soaked gear he's wearing and his insignia, he's recently come on shore, no doubt with General Cota. The grim look on his face tells us that he's probably seen the same hellscape we just experienced. His manner, however, is brisk.

"You boys ready to go?"

"Yessir!" I give him a salute.

Lawrie follows suit.

"Glad to hear. We need every able-bodied man that we can get when we puncture through the seawall."

"Through the seawall?" I ask.

"Down there." He points and, after ensuring that the two of us know where the rendezvous point is, the soldier moves on to repeat his message.

"Through the seawall?" I repeat. "How?"

"Torpedoes, I reckon," another soldier bawls back. "Maybe they got some actual guns off the ships this time."

We end up waiting for half an hour before we finally get moving again. When the line of men begins to move, Lawrie and I follow. Most of the men around me are unfamiliar. Remnants of the first waves of regiments, I suppose. Still, there's no point in waiting around for the rest of our group to join us. If they haven't reached the seawall by now, surely they are dead or heavily wounded.

An explosion reverberates, closer to us than I expected. The torpedoes have already launched. When I get to the edge, where the smoking rubble of the seawall now lies, I can see soldiers with wire cutters working their way through the remnants of wire fencing. The men stream through. A few fall, cut down by the Jerries' bullets, but most of us reach the bottom of the cliffs.

"—take out that pillbox!" I can hear the Major General's distant roar.

The overhead bunker's guns are focused mostly on the incoming landing craft and the distant ships. Further down, the machine guns of the pillbox strafe the beach, attempting to obliterate any incoming soldiers. If we can take out a few of those guns, our boys will have a better chance. It will be a dangerous climb up to God knows what on top, but if we take the bunker, at least that's one less Jerry to deal with.

A group is forming at the bottom of the cliff. Cota's scouts have managed to find pockets of soldiers up and down the beach. Now, consolidated in large packs beneath the cliff, we feel more prepared than before. Men are double-checking their rifles. Lawrie and I have already cleaned ours out as best as we could, but whether they will prove reliable is another thing altogether.

Still, I shrug, *it's better than nothing. We can*

simply go in like cavemen. A gun can be a handy club.

While we sit in our sheltered nook, I light my own smoke and share it with Lawrie. Before us, the beach has become a wasteland of the dead. The abandoned armor, the sunken tanks, and the few grounded boats look desolate. Even more grim are the bodies floating along the shore. In the face of such devastation, though, I feel only a rising determination to climb the cliffs and pay back the Jerries what they're owed. By now, the sun blazes overhead. I am barely able to eat, but I manage to nibble on a damp ration bar.

"Think we'll make it up alright?" I ask.

"We have to," Lawrie replies shortly.

"Yeah. I suppose."

"Look. The destroyers." Lawrie nods.

Gazing over the ocean, I focus on the ships that are now lining up. They look like they might be coming a little closer to land. These ships, a combination of British and American destroyers, had been drawn back previously to avoid the Jerries' guns.

"Won't they get hit?" I ask.

"None of them have gotten hit yet... but someone must have decided that the risk is worth it." Lawrie shrugs. "I wonder if they're gonna light up the bastards over our heads for us. We need the backup."

"At the very least, they could provide us with some cover."

"Exactly." Lawrie smiles as the first report of the guns resounds across the beach. "Now we just have to avoid death by friendly fire."

The power of the destroyers is plain to see. The guns are beginning to find their marks, and shells smash into the embankments above us. Soil and debris rain down. Our attempt to scale the cliffs is now starting in earnest.

After the destroyers' guns fire on the pillboxes, smoke begins to pour out of the holes. One small section of the machine-gun fire has been silenced. With another blast from the destroyers, the bunker and its mortars further down are neutralized too.

With a shout, Cota and his men lead us up the embankment. It is nearly vertical, but determination, anger, and fear drive us. Swarming up in packs, we reach the top and move forward, sweeping through the trees. Those of us with guns fire on the Jerries point-blank. The rest loot the dead for their weapons and follow hard after. The chaos of the battle fades away as my focus narrows to the sighting on my gun and the Nazis rushing out of their smoking bunker.

***

When the sun finally sinks into the west behind the gray clouds lowering over the sullen Atlantic, we can definitely say that we ultimately succeeded. Against overwhelming odds, our group has managed to secure a fairly defensible position on the beach. The few Germans who survived the destroyers' guns have given themselves up and surrendered. Those who tried to keep fighting until the bitter end died.

As the sky darkens, I find myself sitting on the edge of a stone wall looking over the beach. The tide that had swept in now slowly ebbs, leaving behind it a beach full of dead. There is so much work to be done. There is a whole war to finish. There is a country or two that needs freeing. There is a victory to be celebrated.

I can't be bothered.

"Finally," Lawrie says, limping over to me.

Around his thigh, a bandage has been applied to a light graze he got from a young Nazi. The kid had died screaming for his Führer, a horrific sight.

"Finally?" I ask.

"Some peace and quiet at last," he answers.

"Oh, yes, rather," I say with a nod, suddenly realizing that the guns and machine-gun fire have indeed ceased. "For now."

"For now," he echoes.

"No victory smoke?" I ask.

"Not right now," he replies vaguely.

He sits down beside me and looks over the broad vista. It is—or was—a beautiful beach. During peacetime, I imagine that the once-flat sands and the surrounding greenery would have been welcoming for vacationers. Now it has all been spoiled. One day, perhaps, the greenery will return, and the sands will slowly erode and flatten beneath the pull of the water and wind.

"So many... gone," I finally say. "And they were so young. So young."

"Yeah," Lawrie nods. "Vinny. Johnny. Mattie. Everyone."

"I was hoping that somehow… I don't know. It's silly, but that somehow we would all meet again in Belfast or London. But they've gone ahead. Everyone but us," I sigh, my stomach tightening at his words.

"For now," Lawrie points out grimly.

"For now," I reply.

Chapter Six

Amélie
June 6, 1944

Somehow, Dottie and I manage to get Joseph to the Cler farm. The Cler family has always quietly run their farm out in the furthest reaches of May-sur-Orne. It's a two-hour walk on foot, but it takes a little longer thanks to the Germans patrolling the area. Although I used to roam these paths as a child, I'd long since given up tramping around the countryside in favor of the delights of Paris. Yet, here I am, stoutly traipsing back country roads and guiding Joseph around the worst of the ditches.

After an hour of steady walking, we look a bit more grubby and reddened than when we set out. We take a short break and try to keep our conversation light—talking about the Cler farm, what Joseph might expect, the details of his new name, and his new life. We try to reassure him as best as we can about the future. Neither of us talks about the gunfire or what may have happened to the Resistance members and his mother. The image of the stopped truck and the look in Louis's eye haunts me. I can't shake the feeling that Joseph may have lost his mother, but I know better than to speak of it right now.

After everything he has been through, I sigh, *the last thing he needs to deal with is the death of his mother. Once we get him to safety and ascertain what has happened, then... Then...*

It's too much. I can only imagine what it would feel like to lose your parents so quickly. At the beginning of the occupation, Joseph's father had disappeared. I remember Rachel telling me about the night she escaped with Joseph and went into hiding. The two had been spirited away in a cupboard space by French Christians until the Resistance could be contacted. Ever since then, they've been in hiding. Although, now it seems that Rachel's luck has run out. Still, there is a family in America—an aunt and uncle—but getting Joseph to safety seems next to impossible with the recent increase in German patrols.

I can only hope that whatever the Allies are up to, they get it done quickly. The fewer Germans in the area, the better chance we have to help our hidden friends. Almost from habit, I glance over to the west. Now that we are circling around the south of Tilly, we have a clearer view of the sky. The skies are no longer as fiery as they were in the morning, but the distant rumbles have not eased.

As we sit and eat the small lunch Dottie packed, I mentally calculate the distance. We have another hour of walking. After leaving Joseph in the Cler family's care, Dottie and I will be able to make our way home. That will involve another two-hour-long walk unless Monsieur Cler has business in town, in which case we may get home sooner rather than later. It has been a long day already, and I can't wait to get home, sit by myself, and consider the day's events in more detail.

When the Clers' dull brown barn and the gray stone house come into view, Dottie and I both let out small sighs of relief. Within minutes, we are inside, hugging Madame Cler, greeting the children, and introducing Joseph. As young Raoul, the cousin from Marseilles, Joseph will become another member of the Cler household, hopefully, safe through the worst of what is to come. Giving us meaningful looks, Luc Cler asks after our friends.

Dottie glances over at me helplessly.

"We don't know," I finally admit. "Perhaps in a few days, we will know more. These days, with the countryside crawling with the Germans, even the best of plans can go awry."

"The Krauts," Luc says, his voice soft but sharp.

"Yes, they have even come by here for an... inspection, they called it. I showed them everything. We have nothing to hide, I told them. That was true, God help me. But the little one will be safe here."

"When did they come around?" asks Dottie.

"Three days ago," Luc replies. "A small company. We talked, the commander and I, while the squad searched the premises. They found nothing, but they did take my spare tools, the bastards. They poked their head into the kitchen, didn't they, eh, Anna?"

"They did," Anna replies placidly. "I told them to be quiet as the children were napping... and they left me alone after that."

"So, then Jo-... I mean, Raoul's arrival can't be dated if they come around again," Dottie says.

"Yes, they will not notice an addition to our family... and he has papers, yes?" Luc asks.

"Yes. In his pack, in the front pocket," I confirm.

"We also heard from Albert that the Germans are massing by Calais in anticipation of a push from the Allies."

"Calais?" Luc's craggy eyebrow rises. "That would be a tight fit if they plan to bring a large force to bear."

"It's either that or Normandy," Dottie points out.

"Hm. Yes. The beaches. They are well-defended on quite a few points. I heard they have bunkers and pillboxes lining the ocean. Any force attempting a landing on Normandy would end up dead pretty quick, I fear. God rest their souls if they choose Normandy."

"The beach beyond Caen isn't so bad, surely," I muse aloud. "But to the south... Perhaps there might be more armaments. Our friend would know, perhaps."

"Either way, we must all keep our heads down. If it isn't the Germans, it'll be the bombs of the

Allies raining down on our heads," Luc says. "I have a shelter prepared for our family. If your parents wish to join us..."

"I tried," I sigh. "Papa is very determined... and there is his work at the station."

"Ah, he got dragged in, did he?" Anna shakes her head. "Poor man."

I don't want to talk about my father's work. Judging by how morose Papa has become, I know that he dreads the few days he is called into the station in Caen. I try to look on the bright side, but it is more difficult with each passing day to watch my father descend into a drunken depression. The memories of nighttime executions and hunts haunt my father, but he has been able to bring us some information about the movement of the German patrols. Between his work and Albert's blabbing, Dottie and I have been able to discover quite a bit of information about the Resistance. Even so, it is still not enough.

"Speaking of your parents, we should perhaps return home. We've got quite a walk before us." Dottie rises to her feet. "You told them you'd be home by dinner."

"Hm," Luc strokes his short beard. "I can take you partway. The Goulets were asking about a jug of milk if I heard Anna correctly."

"Yes, yes." Anna nods cheerily. She begins to hunt through her cupboards. "We have some to spare for them. Poor things, they lost their only milker a week ago... Do bring them some, Luc. And I made bread the other day. Ah. Yes, here. I'll send some home with you two."

Bidding Joseph farewell, Dottie and I thankfully accept the fresh bread. After giving Anna parting hugs and kisses, we hop into Luc's cart outside. The ride to the Goulet homestead takes some time, but it cuts our two-hour walk in half. Getting out of the cart at the Goulets' gate, we wave our thanks to Luc and make our way back to Tilly.

Exhausted from the walk and worried about the altercation on the country road, we hurry home. Neither one of us seems to want to talk. As we approach Dottie's place, we pause to say our farewells. Our stiff, formal smiles seem falser than ever, but at the sight of a familiar face approaching us on the street, our smiles widen a little more.

The young man who approaches us marches with self-important pride. His otherwise good looks, blonde hair, blue eyes, and high cheekbones are undercut by his pursed lips and gimlet stare. I stifle a groan.

"Albert," Dottie tips her head gracefully. "Fancy meeting you today."

"Dorothée! And the ever lovely Amélie!" Albert tips his hat gallantly.

Fighting the urge to roll my eyes, I also demurely tip my head in greeting.

"Albert. How are you on this fine day?" I ask.

"Fine day?" Albert blinks. "Well, I suppose it isn't raining as hard as it was last night. The worst of the storm seems to have passed, although the sun has yet to emerge."

"That is true," I admit, tamping down my desire to end this conversation right away. "Still, a day outdoors, enjoying the fresh air, is just what Dottie and I needed. It is hard to find a moment for peace these days."

"Ah, yes." Albert agrees. His light blue eyes fixate on my face. "I will say that the day has infinitely improved thanks to your presence. It was going rather well before, but now, I can say that this day has turned out to be quite... productive all around."

"Going well?" Dottie's voice chirps brightly, as though she is hanging on Albert's every word.

I manage a titter, and gasp, "Productive?"

"Well, I mean... " Albert stammers a little. Then he puffs his chest out. "The first half was productive, the second half—more pleasurable, shall we say?"

"I am glad to hear that your day was... productive," Dottie says, tentatively. "I thought normally this wasn't your day to go into Caen."

"No, no," Albert shakes his head. "I was out on patrol. With your father no less, Amélie. And a company of the Führer's best. You will not guess what happened earlier this morning!"

"I've—" I've no idea, I am about to say, but my stomach cramps with tension, and I'm glad to see that Albert is so eager to impress that he has interrupted me.

"Traitors were apprehended on the road leading out of Caen—criminals, part of the so-called Resistance, I believe. Stopped them dead in their tracks, we did." Albert nods with self-importance.

"Apprehended?" Dottie asks, her eyes round.

To Albert, she probably looks like a starry-eyed

admirer, but I can see from the tension in her shoulders that she is probably thinking the same thing I am.

"Well," Albert hesitates for a second. "Since I am in polite company, I will not go into the particulars, but I can assure you that you can rest well tonight knowing that our region is clear of some unfortunate dissidents and their... undesirable company."

"I... see," Dottie manages to get out.

"Do you know if Papa has finished his patrol?" I ask, quietly. "Is he safe?"

"Well, your father is simply a guide, Amélie. I would never allow him to come to any harm. He should be home now," Albert reassures me.

"Thank you." I somehow manage to get the words out. "I think I should return home posthaste. Dottie. It was... It was lovely to share the picnic with you."

We hug, our embrace a little tighter than usual.

"I will see you in a day or two," Dottie promises.

"Yes." I force a smile in response. "I shall see you around as well, Albert. Take care."

With that, I rush home. Entering, I lock the front door behind me and peek into the front parlor, where my mother usually sits. She is bent over a pair of my father's socks, darning some of the larger holes as best as she can. At the sound of my entrance, Mama looks up and offers me a tired, sad smile.

"He's out in the backyard." She sighs.

"What happened?" I ask.

"It was a bad day," she replies. Settling her thick glasses more firmly on her nose, she shakes her head and tuts. "That's all I know. He wouldn't say."

My stomach is in knots, but I make my way to the kitchen. Pulling the curtain aside and peering out of the window, I can just barely see my father in the falling twilight. Just as Mama said, Papa is indeed seated on the lone chair we still have out in the garden. Beside him, a bottle of whiskey stands on a small block of wood. Opening the back door, I hesitate.

"Not today, Amélie," he says huskily as if reading my mind. "Not today."

"They're dead?" I ask. "All three?"

"All of them. You know how it goes," Papa tips back his head, taking another swig from his bottle. "The Krauts just keep—just keep on taking. And what do we do? Stand back and let it happen."

I slowly approach and then, throwing my arms around his stiff shoulders, I stifle my tears in his gray-white hair. The heavy stink of whiskey wafts back.

"Why?" I whisper. "Was it the papers? Or were they just in the wrong place at the wrong time?"

"Not today," Papa repeats. His hand rests against mine. He does not turn his head, but I know that he too has shed tears. "Not today."

Chapter Seven

Eddie
June 6, 1944

The sun sets slowly behind the gray smudge of the ocean's horizon, dousing the world in velvet purple. Lawrie and I have been posted as sentries outside a commandeered bunker, where we have a great view of the beach. Looking south, to our right, the ground seems to rise a little toward the cliffs. Beyond them, other American forces have been landing on another section of the beach they're calling 'Utah.' I can't help but wonder how they got on compared to us, but other than the smoke that drifts along the treetops as it slowly moves away from the battlefield, I can't see anything.

The north doesn't offer any clues, either. The British and the Canadians had their own staging points to capture, but I don't know whether they've achieved their objectives or not. All I'm thinking about is my bed. After the long, hellacious day we've been through, Lawrie and I are looking forward to whatever hammock or cot we can find once we've been relieved.

At some point, we get dinner of sorts—potatoes and sausage with a spoonful of vegetables on the side. Someone seems to have forgotten the salt, but all things considered, I'm surprised and thankful that we got anything edible off the boats. More men are coming in now, making their way slowly through the water. I bet it is tough going, what with all the bodies drifting in the water. You can't take a step without stumbling over a corpse, or part of one.

The earlier reinforcements are already hard at work trying to put the beach to rights: scavenging from the foundered tanks, gathering up soaked supplies, and laying out the corpses.

Wounded soldiers who are able to move to remain on shore, but those who are severely injured are slowly carried on stretchers back to the landing craft. Better medical care awaits in the ships that dot the ocean. Perhaps the worst cases will manage to survive the short voyage to London and get help there.

When Lawrie and I are relieved, our first instinct is to tumble into bed, but I want to have one more look around to see if anyone else from our company made it. I find Neil and Al. They're heading to the makeshift canteen, looking a thousand years old. Slipping and sliding my way down to the beach, I walk a little way along the sand. That's where I find them—Vinny, Johnny, Mattie, and the rest. One of the men is wrapping Vinny up in brown canvas. As the cloth pulls over the kid's face, I can't help but think that Vinny looks like he's sleeping. A few yards away, I see that Mattie has been stretched out in preparation for burial as well. A man approaches my friend's body and lays his missing leg... I turn away, unable to watch. Feeling dazed and battered by the sight, I make my way back up to overhead bunkers, where Lawrie has finally located our cots for the night.

Sitting down on the edge of the cot, I stare at the lighter in my hand. Slowly, I light a smoke and contemplate its flare.

"All gone?" Lawrie asks softly, propping himself up on his elbow and giving me a hard look.

"Yeah."

"I told you to let them go," Lawrie chides me gently. "You don't want to know these things."

I sigh. "I guess I was hoping... " I trail off, then start again. "At least I know now. If I ever meet their family, I can... I don't know, let them know."

"You think they'd want to know the particulars?" Lawrie asks.

"Wouldn't you?" I reply.

"I'm different." Lawrie shrugs. "But most folk, I can tell you, don't want to know."

I think about Mattie, blown to pieces on the beach. Probably a mine that had been buried in the sand. Most likely, he never saw it coming. There would have been a bright flash, fire, maybe, and perhaps a roar of pain... and then nothing. I shudder at the thought.

"Maybe it's just for me," I finally admit, kicking off my shoes and lying back on the cot. "How's the wound?"

"Mending, I think," Lawrie says. "It's just a graze."

"Just keep it clean," I tell him. "You don't want to die of an infection. That'd be the worst."

"True," Lawrie says, pulling the wool blanket up to his shoulders carefully. "After today, that's the last thing I want to happen. Imagine the ignominy of dying from an infection."

For a moment, I contemplate the ceiling of the

canvas tent, wondering whether I'll be able to sleep with the planes coming and going overhead and the distant call of the Navy and infantry as disembarkation continues. But the next moment, exhaustion hits me like a train, and I conk out.

***

Our wake-up call the next morning comes via loud shouts and the general bustle of the camp. More reinforcements have landed. These are the veterans, the ones who had already been through the first war. I was a young boy when it began, but I still remember the hushed whispers whenever anyone talked about the war. It was supposed to be the Great War to end all wars. That's what everyone had said. It certainly felt that way when I was young and watched my father march off. We never saw him again.

Now, here I am, following in my father's footsteps, but after today, I feel more certain than ever that I will find a way to survive. Could anything be worse than what we had just been through? I can't believe so.

Over breakfast, we watch the new men march in. The looks on their faces seem suitably grim. Perhaps they marched past all of the bodies lined up in rows, or maybe past the half-sunk tanks and unexploded naval mines. Later in the morning, our newly constituted company is introduced to a fresh commander. The new leader of our squad, Rob, is a veteran of the first war.

While discussing the orders we have been given for the day, Rob takes the time to speak with us. He is a broad-shouldered older man whose dark hair is threaded with gray. Rob's quiet demeanor and hard eyes speak to a lifetime of war. This man has probably already been through quite a bit. Even so, as he gazes down at the beach, there is a grim set on his lips.

"Looks like you boys have been to hell and back," he comments, folding his arms and contemplating our ragtag group.

I glance around at the company of men that I now find myself a part of. I recognize Neil, Al, and Lawrie, but no one else. Maybe there were a few faces that I had seen on the beach, but when you're under gunfire you hardly have time for pleasantries. The next few days, however, will provide an opportunity to get to know each other.

"We've had a rough go," a short, round-faced kid says, a bite in his thick Jersey accent. "But we gotta get to Berlin, don't we? Teach them Jerries a lesson."

"It wasn't the most stellar experience of our lives," Al agrees.

"Never wanna do that again," another man speaks up.

Rob's gaze moves from the beach back to us. His sharp eyes move from man to man. At the look of quiet determination on my face, he smiles a little. Leaning forward, he slaps Lawrie on the back and nods.

"You've survived the most difficult assault in human history. Possibly. And you've helped to turn the tide of war. From now on, Hitler's days are numbered," Rob says. "But it's a long road to Berlin."

"And Paris?" I can't help but ask.

"Paris will no doubt be on someone's agenda," Rob replies with a shrug. "Not certain who will take that one on, but I can say that whatever road lies before us, the fight has only just started."

"Just what I wanted to hear," someone else comments with a dry chuckle.

Nobody feels like laughing, but there is some small comfort to be found in even the darkest of humor. Even I find myself grinning a little. Lawrie, dour as usual, nods and shrugs.

"For the next few days, we'll be patrolling the

edges of our base and keeping an eye out for any Germans who might want to get their homes back," Rob continues smoothly, drawing our attention to the more important matters of the day. "There are at least two tank divisions being fielded somewhere, probably closer to the nearby towns, although the exact location is uncertain. We have six overlooks to cover and a few other walking patrols as well. I've made up a rotation." Here, Rob consults his papers. "Everyone will take turns with the moving patrols, myself included. Let's see here… "

Once everything is sorted, I find myself paired up with Harry, an eighteen-year-old logger from Michigan. The two of us are slated for the southward patrol route. After shrugging on my jacket, I strap on my cartridge belt, first aid pouch, bandoliers, and favorite knife. Double-checking my handgun, my rifle, and its attached bayonet, I sling it over my shoulder and glance at Harry.

"Ready?" I ask.

Harry, seated on the edge of his cot, raises his head and looks at me bleakly. He pushes a small red-backed book into his pack and stands up. I recognize the cross on the spine.

"Reading the Good Book?" I ask curiously.

"Yeah… " He shuffles a little in embarrassment. "It's not mine. Belonged to Andy. He was a friend from the next town over. I've never… It just feels right is all."

"Nothing wrong there." I force a smile. "I think we all gave the Old Man a shout yesterday at some point. Who knows, your prayers might be what we need."

"Dunno if my words are as good as Andy's, though," Harry says glumly. "We should move out."

The two of us make our way to the door of the pillbox and, on our way out, salute Lawrie.

"So… " Harry says as we walk down the dirt path leading out of the camp. "Paris, huh?"

"Ah," I sigh, knowing what's coming next. "You see, there's this girl."

Chapter Eight

Amélie
June 11, 1944

After our partially-failed operation earlier in the week, I find myself sitting on the back porch and staring out over the unkempt garden more than usual. Today, so many memories weigh heavily on me. Perhaps it's because it's Sunday. Usually, on a Sunday in Paris, I would go outdoors with friends and relax. When I was younger, my parents and I would drive to Caen and attend Mass at the cathedral of Saint-Étienne-le-Vieux. I have never considered myself a religious woman, but as I sit on the stoop, I find myself sending up a prayer—a prayer for my parents, my friends, and the souls lost this week.

Since then, my father has fallen into a morose silence, deeper and more depressing than before. My worried mother looks to me for help, but I simply cannot find the words to say. There is nothing to be said or done, after all. What has happened has happened. Until we find freedom, until the Germans are pushed back, our lives will continue to be a struggle for survival.

So, I sit and chase the never-ending loop of my darkest thoughts. Ever since the war began and the Germans came knocking on our doors, life has been difficult, but the past week feels more terrifying than before. Long lines of infantry and tanks have rolled through the empty streets of Tilly. Our road, which once had barely seen traffic and was frequented only by farmers, has become full of ever-increasing patrols.

What has caused this? Nobody will say. Ever since the day Dottie and I went on our 'picnic,' I have avoided Albert like the plague. There is something annoyingly smarmy about his attitude that always threatens to set me off. My temper, which has often gotten the best of me before, is certain to explode if I see him. And if I start talking... Who knows what I would end up saying?

Usually, after an operation, Dottie and I would receive some kind of word from Henri, but Henri is dead. Summarily executed in the back fields of Tilly. Just the other day, his younger sister went to retrieve his body from the Caen police station. On her return to Tilly, she spoke briefly with Dottie, who passed along the word that Caen is practically a ghost town now. Most of the town's inhabitants are in hiding. The shops are shuttered. Those who can flee to shelters in the countryside have disappeared. Others are attempting to journey to Paris. The rest hide in their cellars and try to avoid the German army that has overtaken the town.

After hearing about Caen, I am more certain than ever that something happened the morning the skies turned red. It was on that day that security had tightened. Our work has now become so much more dangerous and difficult. I also know that I have to be patient and wait for word from Louis in some form or another. If Louis made it home safely, I know that he will eventually try to reach out, even if only to find out whether Joseph had settled in safely with the Cler family.

And what would I tell him? I wonder. We left him with the Cler family. Anna will have told him about what happened with the truck and the German patrol, so I'm sure that Joseph is far from happy. Safe, yes, but he faces another long period of grief and loss... and uncertainty. And even though the Cler family will be able to hide him easily, they face the same challenges we do. May-sur-Orne may be a small hamlet and its distant farms easily forgotten, but to an Allied bomb or a German tank, there is no distinction.

"Amélie." It's my mother at the door. "It's getting late."

"I know." I rise and stifle another sigh.

"You've had much on your mind, I know," Mama says, widening the door a little to let me in.

I follow her into the kitchen and sit down, content to watch my mother putter about. She is finishing up dinner—simple chicken soup with more broth than meat and vegetables.

"Ever since that one morning, things have changed," she says. "Your father is right. Something has happened. The number of tanks rolling through town the past two days… "

"Papa says they are placing the tanks at various intersections of the fields and roads." I think aloud slowly. "Do you think they are preparing for some kind of land attack?"

"Who knows," Mama says with a shrug.

"Albert might know," I sigh. "Not that I really want to talk with him right now."

"He spoke with you and Dottie the other day,

didn't he?" Mama asks.

"Yes. Ugh. So smarmy." I shudder. "Honestly, the man is a tick. He's nothing like Eddie. Eddie was... Oh, I don't know. Eddie was different. He was easy-going and open-minded and—and smart, you know? Albert is half the man Eddie was... is."

"Eddie, the American you met in Paris?" My mother's eyes suddenly light up with a happy twinkle. "You never did say much about him."

"Well, we barely knew each other. The time we spent together was so short," I explain. "We met at a social. He'd been invited as a friend of a friend of the hostess. Most Americans have this, I don't know, attitude, but Eddie caught my eye right away. He spoke French so well! If you weren't French, you wouldn't know he's a native English speaker."

"What did he look like?"

"Tall, broad-shouldered. He had dark hair and

green eyes... and a nice smile that made his eyes sparkle. Eddie was the perfect one for me." I smile fondly at the memories of Eddie's laughter. "And it was more than just his looks. When we sat and talked at parties, when we danced, when we went for long walks in the gardens by the Tower, time always seemed to fly by. Life would never be dull around Eddie."

"I wonder if he's gotten himself caught up in the war as well," Mama muses.

"Oh." I stop to consider the possibility. "Oh God, I hope not."

"Amélie!" My mother protests as she crosses herself.

"Sorry," I pout, not really sorry.

"If he is the man you describe, I think he will be a man who pursues honor and does his duty for God and his country," Mama says, stirring the soup ruminatively. "I can only pray that the Virgin Mary keeps watching over him, wherever he is."

My mother's words make me equal parts worried, and happy. They stir up memories I have fought hard to let go of, like Eddie's last words as his large hands had clasped my own. He had looked at me so earnestly, promising to never forget me and to return as soon as possible. *Surely he wouldn't—! But he would*, a traitorous voice in my mind spoke with happiness. *He would cross the ocean and brave a war to find you.*

A rumble coming from the road interrupts our conversation. Giving my mother a look, I move from the kitchen into the front parlor. Carefully, I open the front door and peer out. Sure enough, a small cavalcade of cars and men are approaching. Many of them look very young, some of them barely sixteen or seventeen. The insignia on their sharp uniforms is unfamiliar, but the poise with which they carry themselves and the passion shining in their eyes are unnerving. Behind two or three army trucks packed full of young soldiers, a large tank slowly rumbles past followed by older, more than likely veteran soldiers. So many men. They are heading west towards Caen, or perhaps the hills along the Verrières road.

I can also see the bent shoulders of my father walking along the side of the road from the opposite direction. He is finally returning home after a long day of work at the station in Caen. Usually, he can find a ride halfway to Tilly, but even so, he returns home exhausted in mind as well as the body. With a feeling of relief, I open the door wider, but I eye the passing men with caution.

Papa sees me standing in the doorway and picks up his pace. Finally mounting the small stoop, he lets himself in while I lock the door securely behind him.

"Another division," he says. "Did you see their uniforms?"

"I noticed the insignia, but it isn't familiar to

me." I take my father's coat and hang it up, allowing him to continue onward into the kitchen where my mother is setting out bowls.

"Who are they?" Mama asks in a hushed tone.

"There's the panzer division and the panzergrenadier... " Papa takes a sip from his flask and coughs a little. "But that division... "

"They were so young," I say, taking a seat opposite him.

"That would be the 12th SS Hitlerjugend."

"Hitlerjugend?" I try to translate the unfamiliar words into my head. "Hitler... Youth? Young people?"

"Correct," my father says grimly. "Handpicked from the most passionate of Hitler's supporters—young people who don't know better. Some of those boys haven't seen their eighteenth winter. The Kraut are sending their lads to war."

"Just like all of us," Mama points out. Her tone is severe and hard in its disapproval. "What times we live in."

"If your friends ask, tell them that the divisions are hunkering down all about Caen. From beyond May-sur-Orne all the way over to La Hogue, along the Verrières road and through Tilly." Papa's hands shake a little as he reaches for his spoon. "I am much too old for this."

"Do you have to go back?" Mama sighs.

"That is perhaps the one thing to celebrate," my father admits. "I will not be required to return to Caen, but I may lend my aid to the commandant who is supervising Tilly."

"I see." I stop to think while I blow on a spoonful of broth.

"I might go in if only to see how their preparations are going," Papa says. "But even if I were to gather any news... To whom would I share it?"

"Amélie's friend, perhaps?" Mama asks.

"My friend hasn't sent word." I shake my head. "And I suppose it is too much to hope for, given that the Germans are camping down everywhere. Perhaps the road between here and Garcelles-Secqueville is too congested."

"Well, if he were thinking to pass through Bourguébus, he would still find trouble," Papa agrees. "At best, he would find himself forced to work for the Krauts. No. I would remain home and stay hidden."

"So then we must be patient and wait. Not my greatest strength, but to even go out and visit mutual friends would be too much of a risk." I sigh. "We wait, and we hope that everyone will come out of this safe and sound."

"And pray," my mother added firmly. "Our Heavenly Father will watch over us."

My father's skeptical grunt echoes my feelings, but I smile and nod at my mother. By the end of this, things might get so bad that even a prayer wouldn't be a bad idea. It certainly can't hurt. That night, my mother lights a candle and whispers a prayer, and listening to her gentle murmuring, my heart fills with hope and worry.

Chapter Nine

Eddie
July 5, 1944

"All quiet?" Rob asks.

He's probably heading for the main camp, but our squad leader pauses for a moment at the quiet intersection where I have been standing watch.

"All quiet, sir," I nod sharply with a brief salute. "No sign of any Jerry... yet."

"Not yet, no, not yet," Rob says.

Turning left and then right, he squints down the dirt lanes and contemplates the view. The road to Saint-Jores is empty, save for the intermittent men on watch. Thirty yards in every direction, a soldier stands guard. Meanwhile, small cavalcades of army trucks occasionally rumble down the road and enter the country village. Golden shafts of sunlight filter through thick clouds and slant through the thickets of trees lining the road. After the bombings, most of the trees have fallen, but a few still stand. Overall, however, Saint-Jores has emerged more or less intact. Other towns, I know, are not going to be so lucky.

"After the trouble, we went through liberating Saint-Jores, I'm glad for the respite," I admit. "It was a good day if a bit hair-raising during some moments."

"Agreed," Rob says. "It was touch-and-go, but it could have been worse. We could have been in La Haye."

"La Haye?" I ask curiously.

"Town to the west." Rob pushes his helmet back to scratch his sweaty, unkempt hair as he turns to look down the larger road. "Down that away. It was a tough one. We lost a good bunch."

"But we gained ground?" I point out.

"Gained ground?" Rob shakes his head. "If you think 200 yards or so is gaining ground... No, the division lost too many in the last push. Men dead. Men missing. Captured, no doubt, God help them. Just thank your lucky stars you weren't in La Haye."

"Only 200 yards... " I shift my rifle from one shoulder to another. "The Jerries are desperate."

"Desperate and fanatical. You've seen them. Young idiots who ought to know better," Rob spat out.

I silently agree. It makes a man angry to watch his boys die and then finally take down the enemy, only to discover that the man behind the gun is barely eighteen. Rob's fury is understandable. Even war-hardened veterans like Rob struggle to comprehend what is being asked of us as we forge new territory in the backwoods of France.

If we thought that we had survived the worst on Omaha Beach, we had another thing coming. Every stand of trees, every corner of every village, every farm lane is a trap. The clean sweep of France's countryside is now a long-buried dream. Instead of making a beeline to the Seine, we find our path continually blocked by the remaining Jerries, who fight for every inch.

"Well, we were able to free Saint-Jores today," I point out. "At least we achieved that. The residents have been so thankful, just like all the others; it makes it worth it."

"And we have hundreds of other villages ahead of us," Rob says gloomily.

"Perhaps as news of our arrival spreads, citizens who can bear arms will start to resist more openly." I offer my commander a small shrug.

Usually, Rob is more cheerful, but today it looks as though he is giving Lawrie a run for his money. I wonder if Rob has more details about the La Haye attack that he isn't telling me. I wouldn't be surprised if that were the case. Still, Rob nods, reluctantly agreeing with my observation.

"True," he says. "I have a feeling that the Jerries won't be able to hide our victories, and the people will begin to turn against them. It should make our job easier."

"We can hope so. Until then, we have to move carefully," I add.

"Yes," Rob says. "We should be moving into Saint-Jores proper tonight. You've got... what, another hour on the clock?"

"Someone should relieve me in an hour, yes." I turn to look down the road behind me and then the road branching off to my left.

"I'll see you then. I'd head into Saint-Jores since

we'll be camping around the outskirts tonight." Rob tips his helmet forward and continues on his way.

Watching my commander move down the road, I relax a little and step back into the shade, allowing another three army trucks to pass by. As they disappear in a cloud of smoke down the road to Saint-Jores, silence falls once again.

Left alone with my thoughts, I watch the dappled sunlight shift through the leaves of the tree behind me and contemplate the road I face. Reaching Paris and finding Amélie has never felt so impossible. Since D-Day, our forces have focused on taking the Cotentin Peninsula, while the British and Canadians attempt to gain traction on our side of the Seine.

It makes sense. Anyone can see how commanding the peninsula would provide the Allied forces a strategic landing zone, far from the Jerries and their guns. Mobilizing from the Peninsula would be a simple matter for our forces, but first, we need to claim the zone, and the Jerries aren't letting it go without a fight. Dreams about an easy victory have long since vaporized like smoke.

Looking up, I see several soldiers jogging down the road at a brisk pace. Time for a change of the guard. One of them keeps running forward, heading in my direction. Judging by the loping gait, it's Fisher. Fisher, birth name Ernest Stanley, is a laid-back stable boy from Pennsylvania who pores over fishing catalogs like they are pin-ups. The tall, gangly young man arrives, face flushed. For a second, he leans over, panting from exertion.

"Eddie," he says, coming to a stop. "Am I late?"

"No," I grin. "You're good for once. What happened? Time got away from you?"

"I was held up by the Commander, who was briefing us on the situation over at La Haye. Looks like progress is only going to get more difficult moving forward." Fisher shakes his head. "So much for being home by Christmas."

"Harry, Alf, and Giggles will be disappointed," I chuckle. "Particularly about losing that bet of theirs."

"Lawrie will probably end up winning the gamble." Fisher eyes me with curiosity. "But you didn't join the pot. I never did get around to finding out why."

"I'm... I'm not into all that." I shrug. "I hope for the best, prepare for the worst."

"That sounds wise," Fisher agrees. "After all, we don't know how bad things will get the closer we get to Berlin. And if the rumors about the Red Army are true... "

"The part about the Red Army taking back territory?" I ask. "Or about the battle in Crimea that cost the Jerries thousands?"

"I was thinking more about where those missing people went," Fisher says.

"Oh." I shake my head. "There were rumors of them being taken eastward, but more than likely they ended up in a mass grave."

"You think so?" Fisher asks. "What about the city the old French lady told us about where all the Jews were sent? She said the Nazis were setting them up with their own county, or whatever they call them over here."

"I'm with Lawrie on this one," I reply. "Of course, we have to hope for the best, but... " I trail off and give him a meaningful look. "After they were forced out of their homes and their businesses, you think the Jerries are just going to let political dissidents and social undesirables live together peacefully? I don't think so."

Fisher looks a little glum, but he nods slowly. "That's why you were so quiet when you talked with her. You didn't want to... "

"Nobody wants to talk about the truth." I smile grimly and clap him on the back. "Otherwise, nobody would be sleeping at night. Better to just focus on what we can do and prepare for the worst. Good luck."

With that, I tip my helmet and leave him on duty. Sauntering down the road, I think about my conversations with Rob and Fisher. It's easy to get caught up in what we face. Men like Fisher and Harry find courage from moral fervor. Others, like Rob and Lawrie, seem to operate like machines, preferring to simply focus on what needs to be done.

As for me, I find myself just wanting this whole ordeal to be over. All I can see are the steps before me: get to Paris, find Amélie, make sure she's safe, and then get to Berlin, free Berlin... and then... what?

I could return to Amélie and make a life, here or in America if she's willing. Of course, at some point, I will return home to let my mother and siblings know that I am safe. I've written two letters, but I don't know if my scrawl has reached them yet. As I enter the village, I notice how the shadows stretch as the sun sinks behind the trees.

Looking about, I recognize the scars of battle— the shell of a cottage still smoking, the bodies wrapped in canvas, and the stockpile of weapons and ammo. Not all of the cottages and buildings have been destroyed, but among those which are ruined, the owners scavenge for what remains of their belongings. A little girl is crying, cradled by her mother as they watch a man's body being slowly wrapped in a body bag. Her father? Brother? Who knows. It is another loss in a war that's caused too many already.

Lawrie, who's helping Cook set up his tent, glances over in my direction. His gaze follows the direction of my own, and he grimaces.

"Eddie," he calls out.

I turn away, lift up the other end of the table, and help him shift it over.

"Nothing you can do, Ed," Lawrie says.

"I know, I know," I sigh. "It just hits hard every damn time."

I remember what I had told Fisher: better to focus on what we can do and prepare for the worst. Time to take my own advice.

Chapter Ten

Amélie
July 7, 1944

A roaring boom rouses me from sleep. I roll over onto my back and strain my ears for any telltale sound. Within a few minutes, I hear the distant medley of shouting and screaming. Overhead, planes roar and explosions boom as their cargo find its mark. In response, the German machine guns and anti-aircraft guns fire back with sharp rat-tat-tats and hollow booms. Sleep is impossible for me.

I shift again and look up into the darkness of the Lamonts' shelter, where my parents and I have taken refuge alongside Antoine and his wife Bea. Over the past few weeks, news has trickled in.

Contrary to Hitler and the German pigs' hopes, the Allies had surprised them with a difficult, but ultimately successful, landing on the beaches of Normandy.

Remembering Antoine's descriptions of the pillboxes and bunkers lining the hills around the beach, I can only imagine what kind of defenses our Allied friends had faced. Fighting under such fire, they had refused to back down and instead, against all odds, had pushed through. The Germans, however, have not been routed. Every inch of French territory is now bitterly contested, and with Hitler's blessing, the panzer tanks have been thoroughly mobilized along our roads and lanes. The abandoned homes in Tilly are now filled with small groups of soldiers hiding in cellars, ready to move wherever needed.

Despite the Germans' defenses, however, the Allies move forward unrelentingly. Caen now lies under attack. Over the past few days, everyone has been on edge, knowing that it would only be a matter of time before the opposition arrives. With daily bombings and dogfights overhead, many of us have been driven further inland or underground, where we hope that we will somehow survive the worst.

Already we have lost people to the bombings and German fire. Celia Manon was blown up along with her little cottage, and Emile Panet was shot in the back of the head after refusing to serve alongside the Hitlerjugend division. I'm sure that Caen has seen worse. The Varin family took in another family fleeing from Caen. Hopefully, their shelter will be able to safely hold them all.

A few feet away, I can hear Papa's snoring suddenly come to a halt as another explosion resounds through the night, closer and louder than before. If anyone was sleeping until now, they are awake. No one says anything for a long moment.

Then, with an audible sigh, my mother rises,

followed by Bea. The two light a candle and set to work boiling some water over the small hearth Antoine has built. Although younger than my father by a few years, Antoine's life as a stonemason had given him all the skills a man would need in order to build a cozy underground home. Not only was he able to section off some areas for our cots, but he was also able to make a small kitchen for his wife.

With the fire going, Mama snuffs out the candle, knowing that now more than ever, frugality is necessary. I turn onto my side and watch the two older women fill the kettle with water from a bucket that Papa had brought in the night before. The small fire now crackles comfortingly, a cheerful contrast to the rumbling overhead. Rising slowly upward, the smoke winds up past the thin beaten-tin shield to the pipe which funnels the worst of it out of the shelter. It is a very simple accommodation, but at least Bea and my mother have a place to do some rudimentary cooking.

When the tea is done, I sip the steaming liquid. Mama has added a dollop of milk, but there's still no sugar. *If we can survive the oncoming war*, I muse, *maybe we'll get sugar back and all the other things we are missing. If we survive... I wonder if Dottie and her family got through the night alright.*

"I might go visit Dottie in a bit," I tell my mother in a low voice.

"Must you?" Mama sighs.

"If anyone is going to go out safely, it's probably her," Antoine points out suddenly. "If the Krauts get desperate, they might start forcibly enlisting even the elderly men."

"They have already sent children to war," my father grumbles in agreement. "I wouldn't put it past the Krauts to drag us out if they thought more men carrying guns would help."

"And Amélie would be safe?" Mama asks, her voice rising with worry.

"Safe? No. Who is safe these days, Marie?" Papa snorts. "No. But she would be safer going out than one of us. Besides, I would like to know whether my home has been reduced to cinders."

"I won't be gone long," I promise her. "And I will stay off the main roads."

Although Dottie's home is usually a twenty-minute walk away, I know that the distance has become dangerously far. Still, I have to know what is going on. After the fateful day back when the Allied forces first came to France, our Resistance group has been driven further underground. Louis found himself unable to leave his farm, which stands closer to Bretteville in the group of towns and farms between Caen and Falaise. I can see it in my head—the map the Allies must be poring over. *Taking Caen would provide our friends with an opportunity to secure the road to Falaise and even provide a staging point for—*

"—cupboard? Amélie? Amélie?" Mama's voice

filters into my thoughts.

"Sorry, Mama," I reply. "What did you say? I didn't quite catch that."

"I was just wondering whether you could pop into our kitchen to fetch that one pan from the cupboard," Mama repeats.

"I can." Setting down the cup, I rise. Glancing over at the door, I hesitate, but Antoine rises with me and makes his slow way over to the door. Opening the small eye slot cut into the door, he peers out.

"It's still gray out," he says, turning to me. "But that might be more helpful than harmful."

"She'll be fine, Marie," Papa says, squeezing Mama's shoulder.

Wrapping my worn shawl about my plain brown walking jacket, I poke at my hair and then step through the door and slip out into the empty backyard of the Lamonts' home. I know the small village like the back of my hand: the forgotten pathways connecting the houses from yard to yard, the cracks in the hedges, and the tree line to follow. Since I am trying to be careful, it takes a bit longer than usual to reach Dottie's home, but I eventually reach the forlorn kitchen garden that Janine had once tended to religiously. As I approach, I notice that Rémy is standing on the back stoop, looking up at the sky. I follow his gaze upwards and notice a neat squadron of American planes flying in formation. At the sound of my boot stepping on a small branch, Rémy's eyes dart in my direction. He relaxes, recognizing me, and beckons to me hurriedly. Following him over to the small ramp leading down to the shelter, I follow him inside.

"Amélie!" Dottie rushes to my side instantly, drawing me into a tight embrace. "You came! You are incorrigible!"

Judging by her excitement, I can guess that Dottie must have some good news to share. I greet Janine and the children and exchange pleasantries with Rémy. I also realize that a young girl and a faintly familiar older woman are also sitting at the small table. My eyes dart to Dottie, who shakes her head.

Introducing myself, I find out that the visitors are friends of Janine, newly arrived from Caen. It is Lillie, a seamstress I had known back when I was a child. After her husband was drafted, Lillie took her granddaughter and fled to safety, eventually ending up in the Toupin shelter. Janine and Rémy wouldn't mind, but Dottie is more restrained around the two even though it is clear that she can barely wait to take me aside. In the end, we leave the shelter and sit in the kitchen, giving us a bit of privacy to discuss Resistance matters.

"How long have we been hiding in holes?" I sigh and stretch. "It feels like years, although I know it's only been a few weeks."

"It has been a long time," Dottie agrees. "Hopefully it will be over soon. In fact, it sounds as though the worst of it could be over sooner than we think!"

"Really?" I ask. "Did Louis send word?"

"A man came by two days ago," she said. "He's been checking in on the group and sent word from Louis. The Clers are... they are still alive, thank God, and Joseph is still with them. The Germans have been too busy defending their positions to look for missing Jewish boys."

"That's good news," I relax a little. "I mean, he can't stay there forever, but if May-sur-Orne is taken by the Allies, then... "

"Yes, exactly," Dottie says, eyes shining with hope. "And there is more. Apparently, Bayeux has been reclaimed. It was easy enough since all of the Germans are focused on holding Caen, but it is encouraging, isn't it? Soon, that might be us."

"But it might take them too long," I fret. "I do wish we could do something more to help them, but the movement is difficult when there might be a tank hiding around the corner of a field, shooting at anything that moves."

"Ugh, don't mention it!" Dottie shakes her head. "I don't know about you and the Lamonts, but we've been visited twice by those pigs, looking for Rémy. He's taken to hiding in the fields, skulking about in hopes that he won't be forced to fight. He is here now to pick up some food, but soon he will have to go out again. Janine tries not to cry for the children's sake, but it isn't easy for any of us, particularly Rémy."

"Well, if the Allies keep pushing, then maybe Rémy won't have to worry anymore. Still, I wonder who will be coming for Caen," I muse aloud, trying not to think too much about Eddie. "The Americans?"

"According to Louis's contact, forces moving against Caen are Canadian and English," Dottie says. "That's the rumor anyway. The Americans are heading further south, cutting off the

Cotentin Peninsula. If they can make it south and cut the Germans off from retreat, or even if they can just push those German pigs back to the Seine, I'd be happy. Anywhere but here."

"Can you imagine the look on Albert's face when his Nazi friends disappear?" I snort with a small, decidedly unladylike giggle.

"Hopefully he'll disappear with them." Dottie's pale eyes sparkle at the thought. "It would serve him right."

"We just have to make sure that we survive to see the day Albert gets his comeuppance. The rat."

The two of us fall into silence as we contemplate the possibility of a better future—a day when Albert and his German cronies get their just desserts when our homes and farms once again become peaceful when I can find a way to meet Eddie again. The window shakes and the glass rattles as a plane swoop low overhead. A few seconds later, we hear the booming blast of an explosion. Dottie and I shiver.

"I better get back home," I whisper. "No use plotting revenge against Albert if we aren't there to see it."

After embracing my friend again, I creep out like a shadow and carefully make my way back home, nursing renewed hope.

Chapter Eleven

Eddie
July 16, 1944

Huddled behind a bush next to Harry, I keep my head low as I look around. The usually calm French countryside has transformed underneath the heavy hand of a storm. Winds whip through the trees. Loose branches, debris, and leaves swirl in the air. Thunder rumbles ominously from the thick, swollen clouds that hang over the region. Rain beats down on the groups of soldiers huddled together.

It is a miserable day to scout, but Company G has drawn the short straw. *It could be worse, I suppose. We could be attempting to attack a village or fight the Jerries like some of the less lucky boys out there*, I muse. *Still, the last time I felt this damp and miserable and confused, it was probably on the beach.* Just remembering the horrors of D-Day brings on a shiver.

I look over at my partner only to discover that the young man has begun to slink down the hedge row. Trying to keep his head as low as possible, Harry reaches the end of the hedge and cautiously peers down the road we've been assigned to scout. After the disaster of Saint-Lô, everyone has been on edge, and if there were any foolhardy men left after the storming of Omaha, they are gone now.

Still, despite our narrow victory, there has been no time for rest. Not really. After a day or so of barricading the city and forming defenses around the area, we were allowed a few hours of free time. Most of us spent it writing letters home, playing cards, or listening to music on the radio. No one had gone for a walk. Any short hike into nature would inevitably end in death or worse, thanks to the entrenched Germans hiding behind every hedge and bush.

The devastating if narrowly victorious action at Saint-Lô, while as important as Bayeux, is scarcely the big win that everyone has been looking for. Caen and Cherbourg are the important locations. Cherbourg is still firmly secured far behind enemy lines on the tip of the Cotentin Peninsula. As for Caen, according to Rob, it was finally captured last week by the British and Canadians. A month late and at a high cost. Even now, while we fight for dominance around Saint-Lô, the British and Canadians are attempting to consolidate their position in Caen.

If you had told me the night before D-Day that it would take us a month or two to liberate France, I might have thought you were the second coming of Lawrie. Now, however, I understand. The Jerries fight like men possessed, I sigh. Every mile we gain costs both sides so many lives. I wouldn't be surprised if Cherbourg ends up just as bloody as Caen. At this rate, we aren't going to get anywhere near Paris until the end of the year!

The thought depresses me, but I know that I can't dwell on it too much. If I am to survive the war and find my way to Paris, I have to stay on my guard and be ready for anything. Squinting through the sheets of rain that batter down, I wipe my face vainly, trying to see more clearly. The road ahead appears empty. The muddy dirt road, flooded with water, squelches beneath my boots. You can barely hear it, though, thanks to the rumble of thunder, the heavy rainfall, and the rustling trees. Ahead, I can barely make out Harry's outline.

Suddenly, I hear a shout and the crackle of gunfire. A dim circle of light shines through the rain. Automatically, I dive under the hedge and scrabble through to the other side, hoping that Harry follows suit. Pushing myself to my knees, I look over and see that Harry also got to the other side of the hedge.

The light, no doubt belonging to a German patrol, now sweeps over the field. In the rain, the entire world is gray and it is easy to hide in the shadows, but the Germans are taking no chances. They began to fire at random through the hedges on both sides of the road. Harry dives for cover behind a wide, sturdy oak. I'm not so lucky. The closest tree is a good few yards off from me.

Now thoroughly covered in mud, I fall to my belly and slowly wriggle along the ground, hoping to get to cover before a stray bullet finds me. My focus sharpens on that one task to the exclusion of all else—maintaining silence, speed, and secrecy. By the time I reach the tree on the other side of the field, however, I notice that the German's focus has now shifted elsewhere.

Who caught their attention? I'm afraid to answer that question. Before I can gain my bearings, however, I realize that my breath is coming hard and fast. Pain is spreading through my shoulder. Somehow, I had been hit and never even noticed. Looking over to the other side of the field, where I had last seen Harry, I wonder whether the young man had survived. I can't tell, and I certainly can't call over to him at this point in time.

I'm on my own. Trying to keep my hands from shaking, I searched my field kit for a bandage, then shove it inside my shirt and jacket, pressing it against the wound. Propping myself up, I struggle to secure the bandage while simultaneously trying to catch any sight or sound of my friends, or the enemy. As my vision begins to narrow and darken with shadows, I realize that my left arm is completely numb. My body no longer responds to my brain's commands. I keel over and pass out.

***

When I awake, I find myself as alone as I was earlier in the day. The storm still beats down, rousing me from my chilled sleep. I lie shivering in the dark, trying to get my bearings. I've been lying there, covered in mud and leaves, for God knows how long. Perhaps my unconscious form had been mistaken for a corpse. Either way, I recognize pretty quickly that I am alone.

Perhaps the Germans had attacked, and our company had been caught unawares. Separated, we would be easy to pick off. I mentally consider the strategies Rob had taught us should we be stranded on the battlefield. The first step is to hide during the day and move during the night. Try to return to a previous base of operations. In a pinch, find a friendly local to hide us or take us in.

The first part, moving at night, makes sense. However, walking isn't easy at this point. After getting to my feet, I fight nausea and dizziness. I feel the bandage on my shoulder and realize that it is soaked through with blood, but the blood is thick and sluggish. No doubt the bleeding has finally slowed or maybe even stopped, but the amount of blood I have already lost would hold me back from moving freely.

I slowly make my way over to the large oak. There, I find Harry's body sitting up against the tree, his face contorted with pain and blood trickling from his mouth. He'd been shot several times, probably by Jerry's machine gun. Death hadn't been as swift as I'd like. I'm not a doc, so I wouldn't be able to figure time of death, but judging by the rosary between his fingers I know he had died talking to the Good Lord.

For a moment, I bow my head, offering a short prayer. I press his hands over the beads and slowly make my way down the hedge row. A truck rumbles past. It's another Jerry patrol. Even at this time of night, I know I have to be careful, and the way back to Saint-Lô might require some finessing.

In the dark, in the heavy rains, it is hard to keep my bearings. After an hour of walking, I begin to realize that I am more than likely lost. Lost behind enemy lines. If I can't reach Saint-Lô, then my next best chance of survival would be a helpful local. But what kind of person would be out in this weather at night?

Still, I press on, slogging through mud and fighting against the heavy winds. I slink through the shadows from tree to tree. After a few hours of walking and hiding, I finally see a building ahead. Is it a barn? A house?

Cautiously, I draw closer, trying to keep my head low in case another Jerry truck or tank passes by. No light shines. Lights at night would mean certain death—a target for our flyboys. Peering through the rain, I realize that I'm looking at a row of stables. Slipping in through a side door, I look around. There is no sight of anyone, French or German, but the sight of hay bales looks comforting. I collapse on top of a row and heave a sigh of relief.

"Eh, you have come a long way, soldier." A gruff French voice breaks the silence, jolting me into sudden panic and instinctive defensiveness.

"Who are you?" I roughly hiss back, also in French.

I pull off my gun. My left arm can't move well, though. A large hand reaches out of the darkness and gently pushes the barrel of my rifle down.

"At ease, American," the voice says. "You are with a friend."

The man steps into the light, a craggy-browed giant armed with a pitchfork. His accent, idiomatic of farming folk, is thick but understandable. His blue eyes fasten on me with curiosity.

"You speak our tongue?" he asks.

"I studied French for my profession," I reply.

"For soldiery and spying?" the man queries.

"For translation work and a government job," I admit. "I'm no real soldier or spy."

"In this time, who is?" The older man chuckles,

setting down his makeshift weapon. "Yet, here we are, brandishing guns and pitchforks. We have to make do, I suppose."

"Indeed." I lower the gun in relief. "I was on patrol when we were surprised by the Germans. Our company was scattered, I believe. My partner was killed... and I have escaped. Barely. Out of the frying pan and into the fire."

"And the fire is very hot," the man says dryly. "Come. Sit. My name is Stephan. Like you, I am also in hiding. The men of these parts, those living around Caumont-sur-Aure, have been in danger of forced conscription. We fight back as much as we can. Soon, we hope, we will no longer have to fight for our freedom."

"That is my hope too." I sit back and sigh.

"I am no doctor, but I know of some who may help you," Stephan muses aloud. "There are whispers of families who know people. People who fight for France from within."

"Are they far from here?" I ask.

"Far enough," Stephan says. "It is a risk, but one I am at peace taking. After all, I could stay here and die like a rat in a hole, or I could go out while doing what I think is right. That might sound crazy—"

"No." I offer him a small smile of thanks. "I actually understand."

"Tomorrow night, then. It is agreed." Stephan rises to his feet. "Until then, let us see if we can tend to that nasty wound. After that, we can plan our walk. It's about two hours to May-sur-Orne, but I know the patrols, so it should not take us more than three. But that is for tomorrow. For now, you rest."

At his words, I allow myself to slump back on the hay bale and sink into the welcome darkness.

Chapter Twelve

Amélie
July 23, 1944

"Amélie, please do think about this again!" Mama whispers, eyes wide, as she watches me pack a small lunch in the canvas bag I've chosen. "It is too dangerous out there—with all those German patrols and executions... What if you get caught?"

"I'll tell them that my mother is sick, and I'm looking for a doctor," I replied glibly.

"What if they take you somewhere further inland?" she asks.

"Then I will escape or go along with them for a time," I shrug. "Look, I don't think they'd try to keep me captive. I am a citizen of France and a woman beside. They won't see me, a pretty young lady, as a threat. Not when they have the Allies raining bombs on their heads."

"How do you know?" Mama says, her eyes filling with tears as she looks at me.

At the sight of her fear and grief, I hesitate a little. I glance at the tall, dour man standing silently by the door. With a sharp nod, he leaves the kitchen to give my mother and me privacy. Papa suddenly appears at the back door, a shadowy silhouette against the gray light.

Drawing Mama into a tight embrace, I wrap my arms around her thin waist and bury my head in her shoulder. Ever since I was young, I have known that my parents saw me as a gift from God, a true answer to prayer for a couple who had always dreamed of having children. As their only child, I had been hopelessly spoiled, given everything that I could want. I could never dream of having kinder and more loving parents. Yet, here I am, putting myself in harm's way intentionally.

What can I tell Mama and Papa? I wonder. *What can I say? This is the right thing to do. I am only following in the footsteps of people I admire. What would you do?*

"I'm sorry," I finally manage to say, pulling away slowly. "I know that in your eyes I will always be your little girl, but this is something I have to do. That only I can do."

"Why can't Dottie do it?" Mama asks, reluctantly letting me go.

"Dottie has other business, with Lillie—you remember, the seamstress from Caen. She recently joined their shelter with her daughter, and there are some questions about a rumor that her husband has been found. Possibly alive." I sigh. "Of course, I would love to have Dottie go with me, but if I have to do this alone, I will. I can."

"I believe in you, little Amélie," Papa finally says, drawing Mama's attention to the door where he stands. "Our little blossom has grown into a beautiful flower, a fierce little beauty just like her mother. Remember that time you hit the Kraut with your frying pan, Mama? You were younger then, and so scared for your little girl. Now it's time for Amélie to hold the frying pan."

"But, Jean—"

Mama stops as Papa steps forward to take her hand and draw her to his side.

"Look at her, Marie," he says softly. "She is doing more than we ever can or will. It is her time to act. It is our time to wait and believe... and pray."

"Oh, Jean!" Mama wails, burying her head in Papa's shoulder.

Looking over Mama's head, Papa looks at me steadily, a sad small smile on his face. He nods and looks to the back door.

"Jan is waiting for you," he says. "No doubt to give you some last-minute instructions. Pay attention. Stay sharp. Be patient and take your time. And... Amélie... do be careful."

Giving them a brief hug, I quickly make my way out, pulling my beret more securely down over my head. I am wearing my best ankle-length walking skirt with pants beneath. On top, I have my thickest, warmest jacket on top of a white blouse. Recognizing that I faced a long journey ahead of me, Bea had given me her best, most sensible walking boots. They are old-fashioned, most likely considered vogue back in the late 1890s, but sturdy and well-made nonetheless. I appreciate the help everyone has offered as I prepare for my trip.

With only a black umbrella and canvas bag, I am ready for what might be the most dangerous walk of my life. Between Tilly and May-sur-Orne, Germans patrol the roads without ceasing as they entrench themselves in the back lanes of France and snipe at the unlucky British and

Canadians who have tried over and over to break through.

I wonder sometimes whether the Allies find themselves as surprised as we are at the time it is taking them to liberate France. Only weeks ago they'd taken Caen, just to discover that further movement was almost impossible. The Hitlerjugend were in part to blame, their fanatical devotion transforming the young men into the most ferocious of fighters and defenders.

Still, I believe myself to be equally determined. Yesterday Jan, one of Louis's contacts, had arrived at Dottie's place, soaking wet and miserable. With how crowded their shelter was, it was an easy choice to send him to ours, where he was able to sit down with Dottie, Papa, and I to talk about Resistance affairs. At that meeting, Dottie had agreed to deal with the matter of Lillie's husband, and I had volunteered to go to May-sur-Orne to guide a stranded American infantryman to Tilly.

Earlier in the war, this would be considered far from ideal. In a perfect world, Jan or even Louis himself would help the stranded soldier, the one codenamed the Eagle, to safety, but circumstances have forced our hand. *In a perfect world*, I chuckle darkly to myself, *we wouldn't have a war, to begin with.*

I know that Jan wishes he could be the one to escort the Eagle, but he had drop-offs between May-sur-Orne, Tilly, and Falaise. His orders were clear, and Jan was expected to finish his visits on time before meeting up with Louis. There is also the matter of Joseph, and whether to bring him with the Eagle to Tilly or not. With a boy and a wounded man in tow, Jan would be forced to move too slowly. Besides, Jan, like Louis, could not risk getting caught behind enemy lines with an American. I, on the other hand, am considered expendable.

And that is understandable, I think as I take the familiar paths hidden behind my house out into the far fields. I am a pawn who knows nothing.

All I am doing is going out to visit some friends, searching for a friendly doctor for my ailing mother, or checking on a friend's health. If the soldier and I are caught, with or without Joseph in tow, we are small losses compared to those with greater intelligence.

Whether Joseph will come along is also unknown. If we can reunite the soldier and Joseph with the British and Canadian forces, that would allow us to get Joseph to safety and his family sooner rather than later. On the other hand, attempting the trip is a serious risk even when done at night in poor weather.

As the sun sets and douses the world in purple and gray, I am thankful for the thick clouds that shroud the moon and starlight. My sharp eyes easily adjust to the low light, and between the increasingly loud gusts of rain, I keep my ears trained for any sound of a truck or goose-stepping patrol. Slipping from footpath to footpath, hedge to hedge, I keep a picture of the map that Jan drew up for me firmly planted in my mind. I had not been allowed to carry it. Instead, I had memorized it overnight.

Jan's observations had noted the patrols, the likely routes the Germans would take, and the roads they currently use. He also had marked where he'd seen signs of a parked tank. According to the Resistance scout, the Germans like to park tanks at intersections where they command a large portion of the roads, shooting anything Allied that comes in sight. Even pedestrians would be marked for instant death if they ventured too close or from the wrong angle.

Still, I have to be careful. I know that every step I take is more dangerous than the one before. After all, Jan's instructions cannot protect me from random gunfire or a falling bomb. His stories of the devastation of Saint-Lô still send shivers down my spine. Hundreds were killed in the Allied bombings. The leaflets intended to warn them had blown away in the wind and landed in nearby villages. The bombs fell without warning, and many civilians had perished in their beds overnight. Hopefully, though, my path will remain clear of any bombs.

Between the Germans and the roaring Allied planes overhead, the path I must follow takes longer than before. When I finally reach the Cler farm, I am damp and tired, as well as exhausted and more than a little nervous. At the sound of the wooden gate slamming behind me, I jump a little, but I take a deep breath and make my way past Anna's garden to the stables, under which Luc had built his family's shelter.

Following Jan's instructions, I let myself in through a hidden plank on the eastern wall of the stables. The wide double doors in front are locked every night, along with the side entrances. However, I easily find the hidden entrance. Creeping through, I carefully pull the plank back down behind me.

Going to the familiar trap door, I let myself down the ladder, pulling the door over my head.

It's pitch dark here, but I keep my breath even and calm as I feel my way down the few steps of the hall to the door I've been told about. Knocking three times rapidly, I wait.

Eventually, the slot opens and a quiet voice asks, "It's late. What is your business?"

It's Luc. He can't see me, and he's taking no chances.

"I've come to set the Eagle free," I reply, careful to follow the phrase that Jan taught me.

"Ah, then you are—Amélie? Oh God, come in! Come in!"

With that, the door is thrown wide open. Luc and Anna, crowding close, draw me in, looking nervously behind me into the shadows. Down here, the whine of the airplanes, the rattle of gunfire, and the rumble of explosions are muffled. A gruff-looking man sits by the table, sipping a cup of tea and watching me with curiosity as I follow Anna to the hearth. Clearly, the shelter has become a sanctuary for many. In the dimly lit warmth, tension bleeds from my shoulders. Promising me a warm cup of tea, Anna draws me close to the fire so I can warm up and dry out.

"We were told that someone would come," Luc is saying, "but honestly, we thought it would take some time. At least a good two weeks... After all, who else is left out here in this Godforsaken wasteland? And who would be insane enough to go out and about? Well, I suppose my questions are answered."

"I, for one, am glad. The poor man needed rest after all that fighting. It's been a week since he was injured, and he is doing better," Anna adds. "His shoulder is on the mend, but I still think he ought not to run about with a gun. Oh!"

"Well, now! Speak of the devil," Luc says with a smile as a man rises from the far corner of the shelter and turns our way. "Our guest probably overhead your entrance... Amélie, meet our would-be savior—"

At the sight of the familiar face—his ruffled, wavy dark hair, his deep green eyes, his firm jawline, and his rough two-day beard—I gasp in shock. His eyes, fastening on my face, widen with mirrored surprise and happiness.

"Eddie!" I breathe. "Oh! My Eddie!"

Chapter Thirteen

Eddie
July 23, 1944

"Amélie!"

I can't help but stumble forward, and Amélie throws herself into my arms. For a minute or two, we hold onto each other tightly, unwilling to let go.

"Eddie!" Amélie says, finally stepping back to look me up and down. "You joined the Army, didn't you? I thought you might, but I was so worried you'd end up, well... "

"Nearly did," I shake my head in amazement as I look down at her.

Amélie looks as though she's survived a war herself. Her blonde hair, which had been pulled back in some kind of a bun, is falling out in loose strands about her flushed face. Bright eyes shining with happiness and worry, she looks up at me, and I can't help but realize how slender she is. Back in the day, Amélie had been a well-dressed, fit woman, but the privations of the German occupation have clearly worn on her. She's lost weight, and the clothes she wears are somber and sensible—a brown skirt and jacket with a gray shawl and a plain white blouse underneath. Still, to my eyes, she's the most beautiful woman in the world.

"And how about you?" I ask. "Don't tell me that you've been stuck out in the countryside? I know you always thought it was incredibly dull. It must be dreadful—"

"Oh, Eddie," Amélie buries her head in my shoulder for a second before drawing back again. "You do what you must, you know? I had to return—for Mama and Papa. They can't face the Germans on their own, and I have to do what I can to protect the people I love. You understand that!"

"I do," I sigh, knowing full well that Amélie is never one to back down from a challenge. "I suppose I shouldn't say anything after my own adventures. I'm just glad to see you alive... and safe and well, after a fashion."

"She was very nearly not safe," Luc says humorously. "But I gather you two know each other?"

Amélie and I glance over at Luc and Anna, who are clearly watching us with both amusement and more than a bit of astonishment. Stephan chuckles, giving me a wink.

"Well." I run my hands through my hair, feeling a little embarrassed about our outburst. "Yes."

"Eddie and I met in Paris before the war," Amélie explains, drawing me down to sit in the chair beside hers. She does not release my hand,

and I cover her still-chilly hand with both of mine.

"It has been too long since we saw each other. I was in Paris, finishing my studies in fashion, and Eddie was there for a bit of a break after finishing his studies in French. But then, the war broke out, and Eddie was recalled to America for his safety." Amélie blushes then. "We were... so young. Making all sorts of idiotic promises, but I suppose neither of us could forget those beautiful times together on the Seine, by the Tower."

"Those memories have gotten me through some difficult times," I admit. "I could never forget... I had to make certain that you were safe."

"You two are... for now," Stephan says bluntly. "There's the small matter of walking to Tilly, sneaking you past the Krauts, and getting you back to your allies."

"Indeed." Amélie's hand tightens around mine. "I was able to arrive here in one piece, more or less. If we are to make the walk back to Tilly safely, we will have to start out tomorrow night. You, Joseph, and I."

"Joseph," Anna suddenly sank into her seat by the fire. "Must he go?"

"He would be safe here," Luc says.

"Yes," Amélie nods. "He would be safe, but surely he will wish to join his aunt and uncle in America. If there is a chance to get him to absolute safety, I would take it. I know that he feels close to your family, and no doubt he's found some comfort from your hospitality and kindness, but perhaps it would be best for him to reunite with his aunt, as his mother wished."

"We can get him ready for the trip tomorrow," Luc says quietly, "if you think he can make the trip safely."

"It sounds like it falls to Eddie to make the decision," Stephan points out.

"Me?" I ask.

"You would be the one taking care of the boy and ensuring that he gets to America in one piece," Luc explains.

"He has family in New York," Amélie elaborates further. "His father is presumed dead, and his mother... " She stops, and a look of sadness and pain crosses her face. Amélie drops her eyes and then glances up at me, her mouth forming a hard line while her blue eyes glimmer with unshed tears. "She was killed too. He's all that is left."

I want to draw Amélie into a comforting hug, but I know that now isn't the time. Besides, I can tell by the stubborn look on Amélie's face that she is fixed on the idea of saving the boy.

"What did his family do?" I ask, perplexed.

"They were... " Anna's voice drops to a whisper. "Jews."

"So the rumors are true then." I glance at Amélie, who nods firmly. "Yes. Well, of course, I can promise to take him to my superiors, or the Red Cross. I am not certain how they would make it happen, but if there is a ship of injured returning to America or some other means, I am sure we can get the boy to America. As for Tilly…" I rub my chin thoughtfully, realizing that my nine-o'clock shadow is starting to get a bit thicker than I'd like. "That is one of the British and Canadian objectives, I believe. How are we to reach them? Is there a plan for that?"

"Well, somewhat." Amélie winces a little. "We've heard rumors that Caen has been liberated, but at great cost. Many people were killed by the bombing, and those left have to scavenge a living among the ruins."

"I've seen that before." I sigh. "It's a shocking sight."

"But France can find its feet once again," Stephan says. His eyes blaze with determination, his attitude also shared by Luc and Anna.

"Yes. I have faith too," Amélie says. "But for Tilly, liberation has been long in coming. The Hitlerjugend and panzer divisions are entrenched in the fields. Too many for the Resistance to handle, and too hidden for the Allies to easily root out. Still, there is a feeling that things are coming to a head, and I believe that in a few days we will be given our freedom. Either that, or we will find an opportunity in the fighting to locate a British unit."

"Sounds risky, but I'll take it." I glance over at Anna and Luc. "I suppose I shall have to say goodbye to your family for now. Your hospitality has saved my life, and for that, I will always be grateful."

"It is our honor and privilege," Luc says with a wide smile.

"I won't say my farewells yet," Stephan grunts, rising to his feet. "I've got some sleeping to do. Wake me up for the milking and chores, Luc."

"Certainly," Luc says.

With that, we separate for the evening. Stephan, Luc, and I bed down for a few hours of sleep, while Anna and Amélie share a bed with two of the youngest Cler children in the second room. I lay back on the down pillow, staring up into the darkness, and contemplate everything that has happened.

Amélie is here. She is alive and well. I have achieved what I set out to do. Yet, our journey isn't over. I have to help the orphaned Jewish boy find his family in America. I have to survive the war. I have to keep Amélie safe. My mind is abuzz with plans and thoughts.

Shifting about, I wince a little. My shoulder has been tended to by Anna. Thanks to her careful ministrations, the bullet has been removed and I am well on my way to full health. Still, it aches and bleeds on occasion. Hugging Amélie had put a strain on my shoulder, a pain I barely felt when I held her in my arms. Now, I remember, and I can't help but wonder when I will be able to move my left arm more easily. Anna said that all I need is time, but time is a precious commodity.

Turning on my right side, I stifle a sigh, close my eyes, and try to get to sleep. I need to be fully ready for the long walk ahead of me—a journey that might not in fact be that far but would be full of patrolling Jerries, falling bombs, and unforeseen setbacks.

Just a few days, I thought sleepily. *In a few days, freedom... safety... and then we shall see.* Slowly, I drift off to sleep, thinking about Amélie and the feel of her hand within mine.

Chapter Fourteen

Amélie
July 24, 1944

The day passes by with excruciating slowness, but eventually, the golden rays sink behind the ragged clouds that still hang over the region. The heavy rains now ease to just an occasional drizzle, and the starry sky can be glimpsed overhead. With many tears and hugs, Anna says goodbye to her recent temporary family member. Luc and Stephan clap Eddie on the back and tell him to take care of his shoulder. Joseph's tears at saying goodbye have eased. Now he stands ready, hands clenched around the straps of his small canvas bag.

Eddie, wearing his mended uniform, looks

particularly dashing to my eyes. My only concern is his wound. Although both Eddie and Anna assure me that he is on the mend, I worry about how well Eddie will be able to defend himself if we are challenged by anyone on the road. Eddie has armed himself with his service revolver, but the amount of ammunition he carries is limited. Besides, Eddie's revolver doesn't alleviate the tension that creeps across my shoulders. Henri had been armed, and he had died anyway. They had all died.

The thought stays with me as the three of us creep along the path back to Tilly. We move quickly and silently, alert for any sound or sight of the Germans—any flashing light, rumbling truck, or tell-tale gunfire. Overhead, planes roar, unloading bomb after bomb across the countryside. Nearby, we can see the burning embers of a row of trees that now stand splintered in a crater.

Carefully and slowly, I lead our small group, followed by Joseph and then Eddie. It's a tense journey, but nobody complains. If any of us speak, it is in hushed whispers, and only when absolutely necessary. No light illuminates our path. Instead, we rely on the dim glow of the stars and the shifting shadows.

As we near Tilly, however, my breath catches in my throat. Large swathes of the village and surrounding area lie in flames. A siren sounds nearby, and a light flashes across the field as three army trucks fly past. Quickly, we duck down. I tug on Joseph, drawing him close. He shivers but remains quiet. Eddie gives me a look over Joseph's head, withdraws his gun, checks the magazine, and then tucks it into his waistband.

We are so close, but it is clear that the last part of the journey might take a bit longer than usual. Moving over to a nearby oak tree, Eddie uses the shadows to sidle upward and cast a look around. He moves down, and gives me a nod. I squeeze Joseph's shoulder, and, bent over, dart across the road with the young boy. We hide behind another hedge and wait for Eddie to check again before he also crosses.

Finally, we reach the small field behind my family's home. Now that we are closer, I can see that a corner of our cottage has been impacted. A bomb had fallen on the abandoned cottage next door, but the blast has clearly sent stone hurling, causing damage to the corner of our home. Once we cross over the small footpath that runs behind the row of gardens, the three of us slink into the empty kitchen.

I lead the two down into our cellar.

"Stay here," I whisper. "I'll be back."

It's so dark, I can't see them nod, but I quickly dart back up the stairs. Once I've located our hidden stash of candles and matches, I return to the cellar and light a single candle. The bare room once packed full of stores and a few bottles of wine, now lies largely empty. In the corner, three cots where my parents and I had been sleeping remain. With my parents at the

Lamonts, the room would be able to provide some protection for Joseph and Eddie.

"The bombardment has begun in earnest," Eddie says in a low voice. "I think your predictions were right. They'll be fighting for Tilly within the day."

"Who are they?" asks Joseph, dark eyes round with fear.

"The Brits or the Canadians," Eddie says quietly. He reassures the boy, laying a hand on Joseph's head. "Either one, they're friends. I met some good mates in Belfast and England. They'll help us. We just have to make sure we find them before the Jerries find us."

"I have to go see how my parents are doing and then check on Dottie and the others. I need to know they are safe," I tell them. I give Joseph a look. "You listen to what Eddie tells you."

"Dottie?" Eddie asks, his face suddenly turning very serious.

"A friend," I explain. "I need to make sure that she and her family are alright."

"It's not safe out there," Eddie says.

"No," I agree. "But I need to know. Besides, I would be in more danger if I was with you or Joseph, but on my own... " I shrug. "I'm just a woman."

I can see that Eddie is struggling to accept my announcement, but he reluctantly agrees. It isn't easy for him, and I know that I'd feel the same way if I was in his position. Just the thought of Eddie running through gunfire to find me makes my heart jump into my throat. Still, I've no choice, and Eddie knows it. I wish I could have him at my side, but with Albert and the Germans prowling about, I can't take the risk. Even now, as I leave the cellar, I know that at any point our home could become a hideout for the Germans. My only hope is that the damage to the cottage will deter their interest.

Getting to the Lamonts' shelter is fairly easy. It's

close to our home and I arrive in just a few minutes. I use the coded knock on the door, and the Lamonts welcome me in. My mother and Bea draw me into tight hugs, clearly relieved to see that I am alive. My father's eyes light up with hope for the first time in a long time.

"You made it home, my girl." He smiles with pride. "And judging by the look on your face, I assume your trip was successful?"

"In more ways than one." I grin back. "You would not believe... but first, what has been happening?"

"We are not certain," Papa says. "I went over to the Moulin, but I had no luck. Albert was away on some patrol. A few hours later, the bombardment began."

"If there has been any news from Louis or the others, Dottie will know," I tell them. "I am going to run over—"

"Run over?" Mama's eyes widen suddenly, tears

welling up. "You are going to go out there with bombs falling on our heads?"

"I need to know whether they are safe," I tell her, stubbornly. "It sounds crazy, but she is one of my few friends, and perhaps they will have news. They aren't that far away, so I'm certain I can get there safely."

"It isn't just getting there," Mama replies. "What about returning here? Anything could happen. Jean, tell her she can't go."

My father nods, giving me the silent permission I was not really looking for. Mama chokes back her tears and falls silent.

"You left the packages in our cellar?" Papa asks.

"Yes," I reply. "For now."

"It isn't safe there," he says. "The Krauts took over at least three cellars already, and they might visit ours. Your packages should come and stay with us."

I glance over at Antoine and Bea. Our hospitable neighbors have already done so much for us. They're only a few years younger than my parents and, like my parents, lack the ability to truly defend themselves. They had hitherto done little to resist against the Germans. To expect them to suddenly take the risk seems unfair. I hesitate.

"If the fighting escalates," Antoine says quietly, "we can run over and bring them in."

"We should do it now," Bea suggests.

"It will happen sooner or later," Papa agrees.

"If you are willing to take the risk." I look at all of them. Antoine and Bea nod firmly. "I can bring them here on my way back. Again, thank you."

Trying to imagine what I would tell my parents when I introduced them to Eddie, I make my way over to Dottie's home. It takes longer than usual, thanks to three new craters and the debris that now bars the path. Reaching the backyard, I can see that their home has been completely flattened. Rémy is standing and watching the flames leaping up from the pile of stone and debris. Turning, he catches sight of me approaching. In the shifting shadows, I barely catch the wry smile that crosses his face.

"Rémy!" I gasp, finally reaching his side. "Is everyone—"

"They're safe. The shelter's held up just fine," Rémy says. "Can't say the same for our home. Still, perhaps it's better that it's gone. Less coverage for those Nazi pigs. Shouldn't you be at the Lamonts now?"

"Soon," I promise. "When I saw the fires, I had to know."

"We are fine for now." Rémy shakes his head. "But I've got a feeling that this is going to be a tough battle. The bombardment may not be enough, given how entrenched the Hitlerjurgend and panzer divisions are. I saw the anti-aircraft guns yesterday. They've taken down a few planes. I don't think the bombardment has been as bad as it could be." He pulls me over to the side of the backyard and points down the road. "Just past where the Moulin used to be, there's an encampment. One wrong move from the Allies, any poor strategies, and they'll find themselves pinched."

"And we can do nothing," I sigh.

"We can hide and wait for a chance to strike," Rémy says. "Go back, Amélie. At this rate, you'll end up hostage or worse."

At that, a sudden scream rips through the sky, and a resounding blast knocks us flat. Scrambling to my feet in the drifting smoke, I look around. Two feet away, a new crater has formed. It has missed the shelter. Rémy staggers to his feet, shouting at me, pointing in the direction of the shelter. I can't hear a word he is saying. My ears are ringing with a high-pitched whine. Rémy runs for the ramp. Ignoring his gestures, I dart back down the path and run for my house.

Another gust of wind nearly knocks me off my feet, but I keep running. I don't care whether the Germans will open fire on me or not. My mind can only think about one thing—the cellar. If another bombardment is underway, I have to get to Joseph and Eddie.

Something is running into my eyes. Sweat? I rub it away and realize my palm is covered with a smear of blood. I don't care. Pushing through the last hedge, I come to a stop, gasping with pain. The ringing in my ears eases a little, allowing some sound to pierce through—the sharp rat-a-tat of the guns, the more distant explosions of other bombs, and the distant cry of voices beyond the edge of our small village.

Men are now fighting in hand-to-hand combat down the road between the abandoned buildings. I can see rows of Germans racing backward, shouting. Ducking down, I look over at what remains of our home. Three walls are left, but one side has been completely demolished. The roof has disappeared. The second floor has collapsed onto the first in twisted beams of wood. My heart comes to a stop.

"Eddie! Eddie!"

I can barely hear my scream above the sound of explosion and gunfire, but I can't help myself. For the past few years, I have lived in silence and fear, whispering in corners, afraid to cry for help. But the dam holding my emotions back releases at the absolute devastation. I fall to my knees, wiping tears and blood off my cheeks.

A piece of roofing shifts, and a large plank rolls away. My breath catches, and I realize that a hand is reaching up. Pushing myself to my feet, I run to help, pulling away from the debris. Eddie slowly manages to shift enough rubble so that he can lift himself up. Beneath his sheltering chest, Joseph lies curled: bruised, shaken, and groggy, but unharmed.

Eddie looks up at me, unshed tears filling his sad, green eyes.

"Amélie. I'm—your parents! I'm so sorry!"

Chapter Fifteen

Eddie
July 26, 1944

The battle for the little town of Tilly-la-Campagne wages on forever. At least, that's what it feels like, hunkered down in the Lamonts' shelter. Once we ensure that Joseph is safe inside with Bea, Amélie and I work with Antoine to secure the entrance to our shelter. Instinctively, we know that the battle is going to get a lot worse. At this rate, either Antoine or I could end up press-ganged into service for the Jerries, something neither of us wants to do.

At Antoine's suggestion, Amélie and I drag debris—wood and sheets of metal from the smashed tool shed—over to the ramp, half covering it and burying it before we enter the shelter. Amélie works silently, refusing to allow me to check the gash on her forehead.

"Later," she keeps saying. "Later."

Hoping the entrance to the shelter is blocked off as much as possible, we lock the doors and wait.

Over the next few days, all we hear are explosions, the sound of gunfire, and men shouting and screaming. Is it German? Or English? It's hard to determine, but nobody opens the door. The risk is too great. Instead, we try to focus on making our food last and comforting Joseph. I tend to Amelia's forehead, and she rebandages my shoulder.

"How're your ears?" I ask, tucking a wayward strand of gold behind her ear. "Have they stopped ringing?"

"Yes," she says.

After two days of pretending to eat, Amélie looks more pale and gaunt than ever. I worry for her, but I don't know what to say. The last moments I spent with her parents feel like a bad dream. We had been standing in the kitchen: her father, Joseph, and I. Her mother had been coming up from the cellar. When I saw the wall buckle in, I reacted instinctively, throwing myself on top of Joseph and pulling her father down.

When I came to, Amélie's father was lying dead next to me, crushed by the rubble of his own home. Amélie's mother dead too, half-buried under the collapsed kitchen ceiling. My mind had focused on a single thought—I'm alive. Joseph's light moan had driven me to fight our way free from the debris. Is this what I want to tell Amélie, though? It makes me wonder what I would tell Mattie and Harry's families if I ever met them.

"You're thinking about them again, aren't you?" Amélie asks softly.

"How did you know?" I glance over at her sheepishly.

"Just... sadness," she replies. "It's... hard."

"Of course, it is," I assure her. My hand rises to cup her cheek, gently brushing away her silent tears. "They were your parents, people you wanted to protect above all else. In some ways, I can see where you get your determination and courage from. They wanted to protect others, too. They were fighting for their family and friends as best they could."

"I suppose so." Amélie smiles sadly then, wiping her cheeks. "I told them that I would come to get you, but they probably heard the mortars and the bombs and... If they had waited if they had only waited!"

It's difficult to imagine, but I know the answer. If Amélie's parents had waited, Joseph and I would have ended up dead. They put themselves at risk to help others, just like the men who fell around me on the beach. To them, I will be forever grateful.

"They were only doing what they thought was

right," she finally sighs. "I suppose Mama didn't want to leave Papa."

"How did you know?" I blink at her in surprise. "She was grumbling the entire time about foolhardy people running about... Something about having already let you go out unattended."

"Yes, that does sound like her." Amélie sags a little at those words. "She never wanted to leave my father on his own. If Papa wouldn't leave Tilly, neither would she. After our last moments together, I suppose she was finished with letting people out of her sight. Now... the home where they insisted on remaining is their grave."

Not just for them, I muse to myself. *If the sounds of the battle raging for the past few days are anything to go by, there'll be quite a few dead when we emerge.* It's a dark thought to ponder, so I hold my peace and instead draw Amélie closer. My good arm curves around her bent shoulders, and I sit quietly beside her, hoping to provide some kind of companionable comfort.

***

A few days later, I win my first argument with Amélie. I decide to leave the shelter alone to find out whether the British have been successful in taking control of the village. Opening the door, I look up to discover that more debris has fallen across the ramp. The planks above me sag under the weight. Carefully closing the door behind me, I push some of the wood back as best as I can to make a large enough hole to move through.

Pushing myself to my feet, I look around. The sight takes my breath away. Tilly is practically flattened. Any home that was still standing a few days ago has been pretty much eradicated. The surrounding landscape is completely torn up. In the distance, I can see a flaming German tank. Turning around, I realize that the tangle of cloth by the hedge is a young German soldier—dead. A few paces away, the body of another man in a different uniform lies sprawled, missing a leg.

With most of the hedges torn apart and the trees twisted and splintered, attempting to find shelter is impossible. I quickly stop to look for a badge on the second corpse.

N.N.S. High'rs. Highlanders? I wonder. *These are the Scots?* It's hard to guess, but I know the dead man can't tell me. I keep moving. There are more bodies, a testament to the ferocity of the battle. Finally, I reach the end of the road. Finding a solitary line of brick and bush jumbled together, I hunker down and watch an approaching troop of men.

Recognizing the strident call of voices speaking English, I get to my feet. At the sight of me, several men instantly cock their rifles, but when they recognize my uniform, the barrels lower.

"What're you doing around these parts, man?" a commanding voice asks, and the captain steps forward. "You're quite a ways off from your troop."

At the sound of the familiar accent, the tension bleeds from my body. They are Canadians, a sight for sore eyes. Although it is highly likely their knowledge of the rest of the Allied forces is limited, there is a chance they'll be able to help me and the people of Tilly.

"It's a long story," I sigh.

"Sounds exciting." The captain shifts a little and eyes me with some suspicion. I can't blame him.

"Name's Eddie. I'm from Company G of the First Infantry Division," I explain. "Got separated from my mates in a scouting mission that went south. Wounded in the shoulder and everything... I've been on the run behind enemy lines ever since, hiding with sympathetic locals over the past few days. Been wondering where my Division would be. I'm hoping I can rejoin them."

"Oh, God, First Infantry?" The captain squints down the road in thought. "Last I heard, half of them got taken out on the beach. The rest are out skirmishing along the Cotentin Peninsula. Isn't that right, boys?"

"Saint-Samson-somehing or other, wasn't it?" Another man pipes up. "After the shite, we've been through in Tilly, I would say they should be sitting pretty."

"What about Tilly?" I ask.

"It's been a rough go, though we distracted the Jerries well enough," the captain finally admits. "Anti-aircraft guns messed up our flyboys good and proper. The bombardment wasn't half as effective. Might as well have been dropping them in the Atlantic for all the good they did. Finally had to go in, and what with one thing and another, we ended up more or fewer pincushions for sport. Lost a good thousand, we did, but at least that gave your friends the opportunity they needed to lead their own assault."

"I see," I look around at the grim vista that surrounds us. In the end, what was left of Tilly was secured, but by then, so many men and so much time had been lost. "So Tilly is under Canadian control now."

"In a manner of speaking," the captain responds. "It's contested, but we're holding our ground."

"Food is running low," I say. "Would I be able to escort my friends to safety?"

"Safety? Hm. That'd be in Caen," the captain says. "We've got that firmly defended, and there are a few houses still standing. How many friends do you have in hiding?"

"Four with me, and another household group of close to eight nearby," I calculate roughly, remembering what Amélie has told me about Dottie and her family.

The captain briefly swears, glares down the road, and then slowly nods.

"Here's what I can do. We have reinforcements coming in, and we'll be relieved. If all goes well, they should arrive by nightfall. Tomorrow morning, gather at the crossroads with your friends. My squad and I can travel back to Caen with you. Well, at least part of the way," he says. "How does that sound?"

"I'll be there. Thank you," I say, with a grim smile.

***

The journey to Caen is anything but triumphant. We leave behind the shattered ruins of a once-prosperous town. Just outside, to the north, Amélie pauses and looks over at a crater that holds the bodies of three men in German uniforms. One of the men has caught her attention—a young man with blonde hair. His vacant blue eyes match the sky as he stares up sightlessly.

"Albert," she whispers. "Oh... Albert."

"A friend?" I ask.

She turns away sharply and follows the rest of

the group, refusing to talk about it. I don't press the matter. Dottie, the Lamonts, Joseph, and the others whisper in hushed tones as they attempt to adjust to the devastation of the countryside. The SS panzer division and the Hitlerjugend had fought to the bitter end for these few miles of land. Even now, they continue fighting for every hill and ridge.

I talk to the Canadians and find out that Operation Cobra, on the American end, had more or less been a success, and the Nova Scotians, at great cost to life and limb, have achieved the main objectives of Operation Spring—even if a few days late and after many deaths. Hearing the news of continued Allied reinforcements landing in Normandy every day, Amélie and her friends begin to realize that perhaps the German grip on France is starting to loosen.

Still, it is clear that civilians and soldiers alike have paid a heavy price for France's freedom. The brisk, if grim, cheerfulness of the Canadian soldiers brings a real sense of liberation and happiness, but it is a bittersweet joy. It's hard to accept the gift of survival when you are surrounded by so much death. I know the feeling.

For the rest of the trip, I can see that Amélie is upset, but it isn't until later, when we are finally behind the solid defenses of Caen, that I can talk with her in private. We find a small patch of grass to sit on while we watch the River Orne flow gently pass. The clouds are beginning to part, allowing the late afternoon sun to sparkle gently on the dark water.

Here, Caen feels peaceful. If I close my eyes and listen to the babble of the river, I can almost believe that I'm enjoying an ordinary day out with my girl. As though people aren't dying from bombs and gunfire mere miles away in the French countryside.

"He was someone you knew," I finally guess. "A friend?"

"No." Amélie laughs a little. It's a sad, shaky laugh. "Albert was the enemy. A horrid boy from my childhood who grew up to be a horrid man. An ass who licked the boots of his conquerors and turned on his own countrymen. I don't even know why I'm thinking about him."

"He was a childhood friend... and he died young," I reply slowly, thinking about all of the dead I'd seen over the past months.

"You don't have to try to explain it," Amélie says, turning to look out over the water. "There's no point in looking back. There is only what is in front of us."

"Caen... and then... " I hesitate.

"Caen for me," she says. "For you, your division waits."

"I hope we can free Paris soon and end this war." I take her hand. Her fingers curl through mine and squeeze hard. "All I was thinking about was finding you in Paris."

"Then, let's meet there." She looks up at me. "Let's fulfill that promise. From there, we can decide where we want to go."

"And Tilly?" I ask.

"There is nothing left for me in Tilly," she whispers, leaning her head against my shoulder.

I draw her into my arms and close my eyes, trying not to see the cratered fields, the crumpled bodies, and the pulverized rubble. War has left such a mark on France. It may carry those scars for years to come.

"We just have to win out," I finally say. "Once we get to Paris, once we clear the road to Berlin... then we can be together and truly free. I promise to make it through in one piece and come back to you."

"I believe in you," Amélie says. She peers up at me, her eyes alight with passion and pain. "Even the ocean wasn't wide enough to keep us apart. I am certain we will find a way."

"We will," I vow. "We will."

FREE BONUS:
EBOOK BUNDLE

Greetings!

First of all, thank you for reading our books. As fellow passionate readers of History and Mythology, we aim to create the very best books for our readers.

Now, we invite you to join our VIP list. As a welcome gift, we offer the History & Mythology Ebook Bundle below for free. Plus you can be the first to receive new books and exclusives! Remember it's 100% free to join.

Simply scan the QR code to join.

http://historybroughtalive.com/

BOOKS BY
HISTORY BROUGHT ALIVE

- Ancient Egypt: Discover Fascinating History, Mythology, Gods, Goddesses, Pharaohs, Pyramids, and More from the Mysterious Ancient Egyptian Civilization.

Available now on Kindle, Paperback, Hardcover & Audio in all regions.

- Greek Mythology: Explore The Timeless Tales Of Ancient Greece, The Myths, History & Legends of The Gods, Goddesses, Titans, Heroes, Monsters & More

Available now on Kindle, Paperback, Hardcover & Audio in all regions.

- Mythology for Kids: Explore Timeless Tales, Characters, History, & Legendary Stories from Around the World. Norse, Celtic, Roman, Greek, Egypt & Many More

Available now on Kindle, Paperback, Hardcover & Audio in all regions.

- Mythology of Mesopotamia: Fascinating

Insights, Myths, Stories & History From The World's Most Ancient Civilization. Sumerian, Akkadian, Babylonian, Persian, Assyrian and More

Available now on Kindle, Paperback, Hardcover & Audio in all regions.

- Norse Magic & Runes: A Guide To The Magic, Rituals, Spells & Meanings of Norse Magick, Mythology & Reading The Elder Futhark Runes

Available now on Kindle, Paperback, Hardcover & Audio in all regions.

- Norse Mythology, Vikings, Magic & Runes: Stories, Legends & Timeless Tales From Norse & Viking Folklore + A Guide To The Rituals, Spells & Meanings of Norse Magick & The Elder Futhark Runes. (3 books in 1)

Available now on Kindle, Paperback, Hardcover & Audio in all regions.

- Norse Mythology: Captivating Stories & Timeless Tales Of Norse Folklore. The Myths, Sagas & Legends of The Gods, Immortals, Magical Creatures, Vikings & More

Available now on Kindle, Paperback, Hardcover

& Audio in all regions.

- Norse Mythology for Kids: Legendary Stories, Quests & Timeless Tales from Norse Folklore. The Myths, Sagas & Epics of the Gods, Immortals, Magic Creatures, Vikings & More

Available now on Kindle, Paperback, Hardcover & Audio in all regions.

- Roman Empire: Rise & The Fall. Explore The History, Mythology, Legends, Epic Battles & Lives Of The Emperors, Legions, Heroes, Gladiators & More

Available now on Kindle, Paperback, Hardcover & Audio in all regions.

- The Vikings: Who Were The Vikings? Enter The Viking Age & Discover The Facts, Sagas, Norse Mythology, Legends, Battles & More

Available now on Kindle, Paperback, Hardcover & Audio in all regions.

Printed in Great Britain
by Amazon